THE
SICILIAN
CONSPIRACY

THE
SICILIAN
CONSPIRACY

Michael Sammaritano

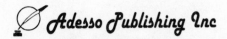
Adesso Publishing Inc

 *Adesso Publishing Inc*

2240 Woolbright Road, Suite 413
Boynton Beach, FL 33426-6367 U.S.A.

admin@adessopublishing.com

Library of Congress Control Number 2006923076
International Standard Book Number 0-9779023-7-4 $24.95

Printed in the UNITED STATES OF AMERICA
0831.5M 393 10 9 8 7 6 5 4 3 2 1

TO MY ANCESTORS,
I am proud to be a Sicilian for we take
care of our own swiftly and
create our own destiny.

—MICHAEL SAMMARITANO

1

WHETHER WE LIKE IT OR NOT, Mafia is in our politics and Mafia is in big business. For that, we can thank one man.

The ride from Scarsdale into Manhattan was a breeze. Even parking was easy. Of course, it was Sunday morning. Eager for news, Ray took the short walk to Grand Central Station. At the newsstand, the headline read:

THE LAST GASP? WITH NO APPARENT HEIRS,
THE GRAYING AND ONCE POWERFUL MAFIA FACES
AN UNCERTAIN FUTURE.[1]

Standing in line to pay for the paper, Ray's mind raced back in time to the gravel pit with the men and machines at work. He had heard a man screaming at the top of his lungs, "Get back . . . get back!"

Sal and Don Saverio were with him on the deck overlooking the pit just as the railing gave way. He and Sal jumped off the deck toward safety. Don Saverio, however, slipped, diving feet first into the pit,

---

1. Associated Press, Larry McShane, November 2, 1997.

letting out a roar that plunged the site into a deafening silence. The operator stopped the spindle and held Don Saverio snug between the upper jaws of the crusher.

Everyone on the worksite, except for Don Saverio, could see the bloodstained gravel and shreds of clothing and flesh falling toward the pit. The snugness of the hydraulic jaws below Don Saverio's waist kept him alive holding the blood from rushing out. Sal, who had replaced the distraught operator, kept them still.

In shock and beyond feeling pain, Don Saverio looked up at Ray. "You got me!"

In the elevator on the way up to his office, Ray was still deep in thought. Then sensing the stare of the other passenger, Ray folded the paper. *Who is he? I've seen those little quivers around the lips, ready to smile. That's the guy; how can it be?* The elevator hummed to a bouncing stop. Ray pursed his lips and stepped onto the forty-second floor. As the doors slid shut behind him, he walked to the break room then to his office.

With the paper under his arm, a bagel in one hand, and a steaming cup of coffee in the other, he pushed the door open to his office. No one had cleaned the room. Raising his right foot slowly, he felt the door's edge behind him and kicked it shut. Making his way past empty boxes and a metal trashcan, he reached his desk. He took the lid off the cup. A few drops of coffee splashed on the blotter. He smeared them dry. *What the hell, I'm moving out.* He gulped down some coffee, leaned back in his chair, and read:

> New York—In the windows of Little Italy's Ravenite Social Club, two faded yellow ribbons dangle as reminders of a godfather gone for good: Gambino family boss John Gotti. The dull fabric recalls a time when . . . [2]

They just don't get it, he thought, dropping the paper to his lap.

---

2. Associated Press, Larry McShane, November 2, 1997.

The more they write about Mafia, the further they move away from the truth. They just don't get it. The longer Ray read the article the more it evoked memories.

It was August 31st, and in Alcamo—like elsewhere in Sicily—the day marked the end of property leases as well as a time to settle uneven scores. No one was exempt. Those seeking a new lease on life had to start with a clean slate and Don Saverio Cremona's blessings.

Carlo had shot his girlfriend first and then his brother, Stefano. The sounds of the gunshots rang in his ears still.

On that fateful night, some forty years ago, the phonograph split the stillness of the night. It played the latest American hits. On the dance floor, the young swung their bodies to the beat of rock 'n' roll.

"Our days, you couldn't even talk to a girl, much less dance," the elders mourned, flipping their noses up like goats to watch the spectacle. "Pitiful." "Rude." "What has the world come to?"

To slow the pace, the disc jockey played Frankie Laine's best hit, "Jezebel." At the sound of two gunshots, the record screeched to a stop. The crowd, the patio, the villa, the entire marina went quiet. From the crowded patio, only the waves breaking on shore could be heard. The only motions were people swapping glances. It was a moment of terror ready to burst. It lingered in slow motion for a few long seconds.

As each step echoed off the terrazzo floor, Carlo Cremona, smirking, walked across the patio to confront his mates. "Tonight, I've settled the score with my brother." Studying their faces, he noted their approval. To further his alibi, he walked over to the other guests. On the women's table, there was a crystal bowl full of greenish punch. The elders had prepared it, for they believed it would fuel lasting relationships. When Carlo drew near, they received him well, but mostly out of fear. Satisfied, he nodded to the disc jockey, and the music played again.

Despite the painful memories, Ray took pleasure in revisiting his native land, even if only in thought. After all, that was where he grew up and where his mother and friends still lived. No sooner had he returned to the article than two quick knocks at the door brought in Silvana.

"Hi, Ray!"

"Silvana, what are you doing here?

"Who did you expect?"

"Oh, stop! I thought you were in London."

"We landed an hour ago."

She looked past him and behind the sofa. He rushed to the front of the desk to greet her.

"Come in. I didn't expect you till Tuesday."

Ray took her into his arms.

She rubbed his back. "I called home, then here."

"The phone rang . . . but I didn't hear your voice."

"I thought I would surprise you. So, here I am!"

"You're not playing detective, are you?"

"Of course not, we're married too long. I might get a little jealous now and then, that's all."

"Smile all you want, see if I care."

Ray wasn't worried, and, in an odd kind of way, he loved her possessiveness. The lovemaking that followed those encounters always gave him the feeling of rediscovering sex for the first time.

"What're you reading?"

"Same old stories."

"Isn't it pathetic?"

"Sure is! But let me ask you, how did we do in London?"

"The showing was a smash. The runway lineups attracted the world's best buyers. You should've been there."

"Isn't it something?"

"*Magnifico* . . . And how did you do?"

"What do you think?" he whispered. "Has been some hell of a ride, hasn't it?"

"Sure has." She rested her head on his chest. "I'm glad it's almost over."

"Let's be patient just a while longer, we'll get there," he said. "You owe it all to yourself. Your resolve got the world to know Giglio as the leading fashion design house."

"You big bull." She tightened her hug. "If it wasn't for you, I would still be in Sicily daydreaming." She dabbed her eyes with her finger. "Please answer my question."

"What question?"

"How did you do while I was away?"

"Oh, that. Look around. Besides the break room, they moved everything else last week. From now on, we can walk to work."

They had moved Giglio's headquarters to White Plains, close to their home in Scarsdale.

"Why don't you have this stuff moved and go through it at home?"

"Too many bad memories. I don't want to drag them home. Except for the books, most of it has to go."

"Ray, I like the way you do things, don't rush, it's early yet. Besides, from now on, I'll have plenty of time for you and the family." Tired from the trip, she kicked her high heels off and eased onto the sofa.

As she fell asleep, Ray thought about how the media reported Mafia being on its deathbed yet failed to notice how the new Mafia had grown more zealous than the old one. *Just watch those congressmen and CEOs and most world leaders and warlords in action.*

From this office, Ray had access to two conference rooms. He also occupied a living room and a bedroom with a shower. The living room had a large window facing east. Until a new building had blocked the view, he could see Long Island Sound stretching all the way to his summer home in Montauk Point. To the left, and if he stretched his neck a bit, he could see his home in Scarsdale.

From his desk, he admired Silvana resting. She was sixty-four and still fascinating. The trip to London, the grind of the show, and the overnight flight had taken their toll. He went to spread a blanket over her and caught a glimpse of himself in the mirror above the sofa. They had both developed a few age lines around their eyes, lines that took nothing away but instead lent character to their faces. Her hair was black and shiny, his almost gray. Her skin tone was dark, his pale for lack of sunlight.

Back at his desk, he swiveled the chair around to face the credenza. Here he noticed more reminders of aging. The frame to the left held a picture of Silvana and himself in their twenties. To the right, there was the photo of Grandpa. The one in the middle showed his parents. The picture was taken a month before his father was killed. His mother had never joined him in New York. Years back she married Sal Rocca. Sal was Ray's most trusted man. In the corner of the office sat an old Olivetti on its own stand, the carriage held a yellowed sheet of paper with two faded lines.

Frustrated with the new building, he kept the curtains behind him shut. Looking back at Silvana, his thoughts drifted back to that last party at Alcamo Marina.

Ray had been sitting alone on the patio, facing the sea. He was twenty years old and concerned about the decision he was making. To avenge his father, he would join Don Saverio. He would put his dream of becoming a novelist on hold for a while. This last thought took him back to a few days before his father was killed.

Roaming about the house, little Ray peeked into his mother's studio. In front of a sunlit window, there was the monster. On many nights, he heard it shoot those rapid tic-tic-tics. Daringly, he approached it. At eye level, he saw an arena of black seats with white letters on them. He stepped closer and touched one of the seats on the far left. But nothing happened. When he pressed harder, a lever with a hammerhead came loose, speeding up to the center gate as a ribbon lifted, as though to protect the paper. The hammer smashed down on the ribbon anyway, leaving the letter "A" behind.

Little Ray was mystified. It was fun. Then he pressed the Z, and the C, and the V, and the M, and the M again, and then the Q. But when he pressed the "Tab," havoc struck. The carriage rushed left, striking a bell that reverberated through his ears to his head and out of his body, leaving Little Ray in shock. The ring got his mother's attention. Scared of the monster, he stepped back and waited, thinking. When he thought it was safe, he moved closer again as his mother, coming to his aid, reached from behind and slid the paper up a notch. Then she took his finger and helped him pound out eight more letters:

R-a-y G-r-e-c-o

"What's that, Mama, what's that?"

"It's your name."

"My name, Mommy? My name?" he giggled, looking up at her.

His mother taught Ray how to read and type. As a teenager, although a genius and bored to death in school, he became an avid reader and then a writer who published essays that attracted attention.

A few years later, one Sunday after Mass, Ray was talking with Father Francesco. Steered by Silvana, Don Saverio joined them. She wore a yellow polka-dot dress. Her radiant smile fit the encounter.

"Don Saverio, I want you to meet Ray Greco," said Father Francesco.

"Pleased to meet you, Ray."

Silvana smiled, as her father reached for Ray's hand while glancing at her. "Papa, Ray writes those essays you love so much in the *Gazzetta*."

"I like your writing, young man. Come visit me sometime. I would like to share some thoughts with you."

"How's Tuesday?"

Don Saverio leaned on his cane. "That's just fine."

The thought of Ray coming to the house excited Silvana. They might get to talk alone. Regardless, she knew this was the start of something good. Oblivious to it all, Father Francesco looked on smiling, sporadically twitching his nose.

Now, eight years later, Ray had decided to join Don Saverio. As usual, he was sitting on the patio listening to the music instead of partying. He enjoyed watching the marina as the breeze whipped across his face. Tonight he couldn't tell the sky from the sea. The lamps on the fishing boats were blending with the stars above. It was a cosmic show.

Alcamo Marina is nature's stage where people party until dawn on summer nights. Tonight was the season's last party. And before Ray left for America, he had to win over Silvana.

Between songs, Ray heard a girl howling. The sound came from near the garden shack whence the two gunshots had echoed just earlier in the evening.

Breaking away from his thoughts and looking across the desk, he admired Silvana. He was a happy man. She was his partner. She was also the mother of his three children. She had given him many wild moments without ever howling. Glancing at her sensual body, he suddenly had the urge to pack. He wanted to make it home before Sunday dinner with the kids. He set an empty box on the desk and the trashcan by his side.

The tinkle of a master key attached to a silver dollar striking the bottom of the trashcan brought to mind the kid from Harman Street and Santo Pellegrino. "The guy in the elevator," he said loud enough to wake Silvana.

"Son of a bitch—That's him all grown up now, do you imagine? Maybe he didn't recognize me either. I swear I'll get him. . . . I'm sorry. I didn't mean to wake you. I'll be through in a bit; I'd like to get home before the kids do."

"Me, too," she stretched and smiled.

Ray pushed the box aside, approached the sofa, and reached out for her. "Why wait?"

Relaxed now, they were both ready to go home.

"Ray, what really happened to my father? . . . Did he ask for me? I thought Sal had it all under control?"

2

ALCAMO MARINA LIES ON SICILY'S NORTHERN SHORE, on the Tyrrhenian Sea a few miles north of Alcamo and just east of Castellammare del Golfo. It stretches from the sea halfway up a six-hundred-foot hill. Its four miles of coastline are crowded with bungalows and villas, but nothing in the chaotic landscape takes away from the beauty of the sandy white beach. Rather, it adds color to the scene.

If you swim out awhile and look back, past and over the hill, in the background you'll see a rustic square tower atop a mountain. It's Alcamo's most prominent landmark, Torre Saracena. The mountain is the 2,600-foot Monte Bonifato.

Every year, from school closing to mid-September, Alcamo Marina becomes a nonstop playground for the young and a vacation bonanza for their mothers. It's tradition that families migrate to the beach while husbands and fathers continue to work every day to support their families' time of leisure.

In Sicily, going to school beyond the fifth grade wasn't the norm until the fifties. It wasn't for lack of schools; there were several fine ones. It was for lack of real purpose. It was celebrities like Frank Sinatra, Elvis Presley, Errol Flynn, Humphrey Bogart, Fred Astaire, and many others who turned things around.

Young Sicilians started dreaming of becoming singers, dancers, movie stars, even tough guys. Dreams, they thought, that could only come true in faraway lands. Responding to that mind-set, the school board promoted education as the "in" thing.

With diplomas in hand, the young sought visas to enter the United States permanently. Those unable to get visas migrated to other countries to enter the United States later as residents of that country. To give these young men a head start, the school board set up vocational schools in many cities. Here, besides learning a trade, a student would also learn how to compete for better jobs in foreign markets.

The program had three objectives: get the students greater global acceptance, pave the road for those who followed, and cut down unemployment at home.

Unbeknownst to the promoters, it took Don Saverio more than ten years to manipulate them into planning and implementing that program. And because of his ties with business tycoons and heads of state, he stood in the background aggressively reforming Mafia to its original ideology.

In all his fifty years, Don Saverio never made headlines. According to the locals, he never traveled beyond Sicily. When he looked at you, his smile either sent chills down your spine or uplifted your spirit. He loved to limp around leaning on a cane, claiming it helped him carry his six-foot frame. The truth was that, in his hands, the cane was a deadly weapon.

Ray Greco was home, getting things ready for his move to New York. In his room, he could hear the sizzling from a frying pan. When the smell of fresh tomato sauce became irresistible, he followed it to its source. On the stove were a frying pan and two steaming pots. His mother stood in front of them like an orchestra leader. She held a wooden spoon in one hand and a fork in the other. The larger of the pots was full of boiling water, waiting for the pasta. The sauce was ready to complement the best gourmet dinner money could buy. Approaching his mother from behind, Ray wrapped his arms around her.

"I'll miss you."

"Sure . . . sure!"

She flipped a cutlet.

"For real, Ma!"

"Good talk, son, and who's going to do your laundry? Tell me, who?"

Ray soaked a piece of bread in the sauce. "I'll send it back here or do it myself. Better yet, I'll marry the cleaning lady."

She screwed up her face. Ray licked his lips clean.

"For God's sakes, Ma, stop worrying. I'll be all right, you'll see. Besides, you'll be there before you know it."

No one could care for Ray but his mother. She even barred the house cleaner from doing his laundry.

Ray was an educated young man with strong beliefs and a winning smile. Despite his imposing build, just over six feet with wrists as big as other men's arms, he would only use his smile and good sense to make a point. But what fascinated people most about Ray was his narrow streak of white hair. Those who knew him claimed the streak was a sign of rare intellect, the root of his genius. Others, especially old women, placed the blame squarely on his father for failing to satisfy his wife's desires while she was pregnant. His mother was convinced it was a sign that the gods had selected her son for a purpose not yet known; nevertheless, she nurtured feelings that concerned her greatly.

Since the loss of her husband, Ray was Francesca's only family. As most children do, he did not think of his mother as a young woman. Nor did he think of her as beautiful. He assumed that her slender body, light-brown hair, and blue eyes were ordinary. To his credit, though, he conceded that her suffering had worn down her smile.

Francesca had been a teacher from Northern Italy. The traditional Greco family had never accepted her marrying their son while he was serving in the military away from home. The Grecos hadn't had the chance to approve her as family and did not go to the wedding, no less view the bloodstained bed sheets the morning after to prove her virginity.

"Who the hell is she? She's a whore!"

For her son's sake, Francesca had adopted most Sicilian customs. However, it didn't work: she never lost her northern dialect, and the

Grecos never appreciated her efforts. This strained relationship had also built a barrier between Ray and Grandpa Greco.

She pulled her son closer and stared in his eyes. "If your father were alive, you'd be going nowhere, young man."

He stood at attention like a soldier facing his drill sergeant, then he mustered enough courage to stand at ease. "Ma! How many times do I have to say it? I promise I'll send for you as soon as I settle down and my papers are in order. Besides, Don Saverio is behind me, rock solid."

"Sure," she bit her lower lip and nodded at the mention of Don Saverio. Ray knew then that she had just locked herself into secrecy. As he held her in his arms, she whispered, "Trust nobody, not even your mother!"

"But I trust him! He's the father I never—"

A tear rolled down her cheek cutting his sentence short and forever changing his life. From that moment forward, he thought of his father's death as no accident, and, as his mother said, he trusted nobody, not even her— no less Don Saverio. Ray was committed to drive himself blindly into the future, and Don Saverio's family became his port of entry to a world of intrigue and deception he couldn't ever have imagined. That was Ray Greco's last dinner at home.

Luciano Greco was a road contractor. Aware of his son's traits, he wanted to reinforce his character with firsthand experiences. On that day, father and son hopped in the car and pulled out of the garage. "Where would you rather go, to the beach or visit job sites?"

Little Ray just gazed into the side-view mirror.

It wasn't until he glimpsed the beach twenty minutes into the ride that he looked up at his father. His shining little eyes said it all. He was terribly disappointed. Luciano pulled off the road and nosed the car toward a roadside bench. He parked the car, shut the engine off, and stretched out a hand to fix his son's short trousers and suspenders. Then, with the sun at about noon, they got out, walked to the bench, and sat facing the sea.

Little Ray made a pass at a fly buzzing to his right. It droned away. There was silence until a tingling on his lap drew his attention. There it was, brushing its head over and again, on seemingly borrowed time. He looked at the fly for a while as if it were an airplane refueling; then, sensing his father's stare, Ray waved it away once more.

His father kicked a lump of weeds from under his feet. "Ray, in life you've got to make up your own mind."

He kicked another lump. "When the choice is yours to make, you must choose. If you don't, someone else will choose for you. Like to-day, chances are you'll wind up where you don't want to be."

He kicked one more. "Don't forget, son, never let others decide for you. Right or wrong, you must make your own decisions."

Luciano rose to his feet and walked behind the bench. Although tempted to pat Ray's back, he did not spoil the moment.

Little Ray looked down, swinging his dangling feet back and forth, stretching the shadow of his legs longer and shorter and thinking about what his father had said. Then, looking at the sea, he rubbed his white streak of hair twice.

Luciano was proud. He knew Ray had learned a lesson.

Jumping to his feet and holding hands with his father, Little Ray walked to the beach to watch the waves lapping on the shore.

Ray got his feet wet. "Look, Papa, from here I can see the other side of the sea."

"No, Ray. The other side of the sea is too far out for you to see."

"Then what is it, what is it?"

"That's the horizon."

"What's horizon, Papa?"

"The horizon is where the sky seems to touch the earth. About thirteen miles out, and that's the furthest point a man can see from here on a clear day."

Ray squinted at his father. "Oh, I see, I see now . . . like you showed me once with the big balloon, remember?"

"That's right!"

"Because the world is round," Ray formed a circle over his head with his arms, "the only way you can see further is getting up higher like birds do, right, Papa?"

Little Ray was rubbing his streak of white hair once more.

Often, Ray's parents questioned whether this action was a habit or a natural reaction to stimulate his memory. Regardless, they thought he was developing a good attitude about doing things others would not, or could not, do.

Later that week, Ray went job-hopping with his father. The two-inch gravel for roadbeds was hand-crushed by the roadside by gangs of pieceworkers. Each worker, with a straw pillow to sit on and a double-headed hammer, relentlessly cracked stones from sunup to sundown. On both sides of the road ahead, there were endless mounds of rocks, each with a pieceworker atop, enveloped in a liquid heat wave. What little Ray saw, though, were vultures on a kill tearing at remains others had left behind.

The hammering, at first faint, sounded like thousands of crickets out of sync, growing louder as he and his father drew near. The car stopped at the first mound. The worker facing away stopped hammering but did not rise or look back. Little Ray climbed the mound quietly, sprang onto the worker's back, and blindfolded him with his little hands.

"Peek-a-boo, guess who?"

"I don't know, who?"

"Ray, Uncle Sal. It's me, Ray!"

He giggled his way onto Uncle Sal's lap.

"Oh no, it's you again!"

Sal Rocca was the lead man for the pieceworkers. At twenty-nine, he was a year older than Luciano. Ray's trick panned out every time, for he always found another wooden soldier in Sal's shirt pocket. Thus far, he had collected a forty-piece squad complete with a captain on horseback and five vanguards aiming on one knee ready to shoot. The set was the envy of his friends. Ray always cherished these moments with his father and Sal. He loved them both dearly.

In 1951, as part of the new educational program, the school board opened a vocational school in Alcamo. The first year's enrollment was just short of one hundred students. By 1956, it was a wonder that out of a bunch of kids who had been so opposed to going to school, eighty-six graduated. What had kept them focused was their resolve to break into the world in style, a trait other nations rarely encouraged their students to develop. Don Saverio always thought of this as a great asset to his plan.

Although Don Saverio was interested in all the graduates, as a debut for his master plan, he handpicked three students from the vocational school and eight from the high school. He groomed them personally for the roles he was preparing them to play. His son, Carlo, was a special addition to the group.

As they developed the skills to carry out his goals, Don Saverio breathed easier. Like thoroughbreds, his protégés were standing nervously at the starting gate, eager to race in the fast lanes of life. He was confident that at the right time he could pass the torch to his next-in-line risk-free, for these students would support his heir unconditionally. These thoroughbreds were the Class of '56.

There was no doubt that Don Saverio Cremona was the head of Mafia. There was also no doubt that he averted the end of Mafia. Except for his son, Carlo, this was the Class of '56's last summer in Alcamo. Because they had common cause, its members developed an unbreakable bond. While the Class of '56 worked on counseling those Mafia families willing to reform to his ideology, Don Saverio set about dismantling those unwilling by planting destructive moles in their midst. These moles, by design, had no links with the Class of '56. They were Don Saverio's power base and his most trusted men.

It was the wee hours of the morning, and the party had dwindled. Two police officers were looking into the earlier shooting. So far, all they learned was that no one saw a thing. Rumor had it that Stefano, shamed for having an affair with Carlo's girlfriend, Gloria, shot her and then himself.

Ray was sitting at the edge of the patio as usual. Carlo was waiting at the far side to start a meeting with the Class of '56 when the officers walked his way. The elder drew closer. "I'm sorry about your brother. The evidence is still there, if you care to see it before we move the bodies. He's still holding the shotgun. It's only up the hill."

Carlo looked away. "No. I don't think I can bear the sight. I'll drive up to my parents' home at daybreak. I'd like to break the news myself."

The officer looked at his partner. "We'll keep it quiet until noon. Please give our condolences to your father."

Angelo and Victor were the first to arrive. They walked toward Ray, casually. To his surprise, neither said a word. They stood by quietly. As the others arrived, they also sat along the edge in silence. Perched like roosters waiting for the first rays to break through the sky, they just waited.

Identifying with their ordeal, Ray wondered. *Are these people still in shock or unmoved by it all? If the shooting tonight was the test Don Saverio always talked about, they all passed it with flying colors. No one even blinked.* He broke the silence. "So, Victor, how was Gina?"

"It's none of your business!"

Victor stared at the others. "What are you laughing at?"

"Victor . . . how was Gina? And don't give me any hogwash, we're all ears."

Victor bent over to shake the sand out of his curly hair that he had collected from lying on his back. "Like the others. She was nervous at first, but then wild and crazy. Why even ask? I'm sure you all heard her loud and clear."

"How could she do that? I thought for sure the gunshots scared the living daylights out of her." Ray refrained from asking what the secret of making girls howl was.

"She was shaken up at first, but when I got there after the shooting, she came running. And you heard the rest."

Victor Como, nineteen, barely stood five-six. When he talked, his thin lips parted just enough to let the words slip out. He feared nothing, and while most men feared him, the girls loved him. He blamed his sex appeal. Others believed girls were after him because he was well-endowed. To play it safe, he didn't wait for girls to seek him out; he chased the ones he liked and the ones who played hard to get.

Angelo shook his head. "Victor, I thought you knew Ray by now. I'll bet he didn't hear a thing. He's like Don Saverio: once on your case, he'll look straight through you leaving no place to hide."

Ray smiled. "Look, Angelo, you're not too shabby yourself. I heard Gina from start to end."

Angelo Sutera, also nineteen, had the same physique as Victor. His eyes sparkled with fervor.

Another classmate intervened.

"Ray, how did you know it was Victor? How did he sound?"

"No. I never heard him. He was the only one missing."

With daybreak approaching, Carlo, four to five years older than the rest, herded everyone to the middle of the patio. "Okay, listen up. In the future, our mission will prevent us from gathering together in one place. We've known each other most of our lives, and thanks to my father's teachings, we are better than brothers. Our bond will always go beyond Christmas dinners and birthday celebrations and any future family ties we might develop."

The twelve young men formed a circle.

"This bond will stand forever above any other obligation we undertake. Although we will part, we must always remain loyal to one another, for we are one. And when one hurts, we all hurt."

Like spokes in a wheel that are bonded at the hub, they held hands as a falling star streaked across the Sicilian sky proclaiming its approval.

3

IN ALCAMO, THE RULES WERE CLEAR: If you killed yourself, your family could not have you laid out for viewing, the church would not grant you a funeral service, and the coroner would take your body directly to the mortuary. The only ceremony allowed, if your family so chose, was a brief one at the burial site.

The Cremona family laid Stefano in the guest room. He was propped up in a dark gray suit, white shirt, and tie. A new pair of black shoes with shiny brown soles, like elongated mirrors, faced all comers squarely. To help disguise his damaged skull, his head was halfway sunk in a thick pillow. His face had been expertly repaired with skin-colored wax, giving him a peaceful look that was only somewhat sufficient to comfort his mother's distress.

Donna Maria looked on then leaned toward Silvana. "Your father doesn't believe your brother killed himself. He promised to get to the bottom of it; he promised."

"He will, Mama; believe me, he will."

Two massive candelabras stood at the foot of the bed like guardians of the dead. Each gave off undulating black smoke that spotted the white ceiling just as sins brand the soul. Eight freestanding flower garlands were placed about the room, each with a golden ribbon on which black letters spelled out the donor's name. Other bouquets were piled up at the base of the candelabras, around the bed, and outdoors.

The smell of burning wax mixed with the fragrance of the flowers choked the air with that unique smell associated with funerals that lingers in one's memory. Around the bed sat Stefano's immediate family and friends, teary-eyed. They all were dressed in black from head to toe.

Donna Maria, Silvana, and Don Saverio's two sisters, Laura and Nina, sat to the left. Don Saverio's sisters-in-law, Carmelo's and Gaspare's wives, sat directly behind them. Except for Silvana, these women seemed experienced at weeping to a beat. They moaned in harmony and often cried aloud to the surprise of the onlookers.

Squeezing her mother's hand, Silvana looked for familiar faces. She nodded to them in appreciation. Eyeing her mother's agonized face, she thought, how can I tell her about Gloria with Stefano's baby, and Carlo marrying her in December? Carlo did what any man of honor would do. The family couldn't endure such shame.

Aunt Laura, between bursts of sobs, leaned back toward her sisters-in-law and whispered, "He was such a nice boy."

"Carmelo can't believe it either."

Carmelo's wife leaned forward. "I know, Carmelo is in shock. He's going to look into it also."

Their whispers weren't soft, except for Silvana's; they all nodded at the same time.

To the right side of the bed, there were two rows of chairs reserved for latecomers and acquaintances who only wished to make a brief appearance. Any other seat, except Don Saverio's chair and that of his two brothers at the head of the bed, was fair game for those wishing to prolong their visit.

Don Saverio spent most of the morning in his studio with his brothers accepting condolences from friends. His plain mahogany desk stood foursquare and sturdy on the two-toned marble floor. It said plainly, "If you've nothing to do, don't do it here." The morning paper rested on its polished surface. The lead article read:

Stefano Cremona Dies of Brain Tumor

Don Saverio Cremona's older son died last night despite emergency brain surgery . . .

Father Francesco did not only spin the media, but arranged a first class funeral in church. To Father Francesco, the Cremonas were not common people. Their donations always topped those of any other churchgoer.

Carlo climbed the stairs and walked into his father's studio breathing heavily. "The hearse is here!"

His uncle, Carmelo, stared at him. "What's the hurry, Carlo? Stefano's dead. And dead people cannot be hurried."

Carlo stared back at his five-foot-four, husky, squared-faced uncle.

Sensing hostility, Don Saverio drew his brother's attention to an unframed photograph. It showed Stefano holding four-month-old Silvana in her bath. Carmelo passed the photo to Gaspare and back to Don Saverio, who then slipped it back in the drawer. Gaspare, contrary to Carmelo, was much taller than his brothers with a deceptive smile that led you to believe he was always confused but focused on his beliefs.

"Are Ray and Victor here yet?" asked Don Saverio.

"Yes. And so are the others. The room is packed with people." Carlo reflected on his uncle's words as each uncle hugged and patted his father on the back.

With his cane in one hand and grasping Carlo's arm with the other, Don Saverio followed his brothers out of the study with a rare and disturbing smile. They came down the marble stairs under the gaze of a room full of people. Carmelo and Gaspare headed for their seats. Don Saverio led Carlo to an empty chair next to Ray. Then, like an appraiser, he circled Stefano's body once and sat between his two brothers. Ray looked at Don Saverio and thought, the king of the jungle has circled the kill.

Staring at his feet, with both hands on his cane and an occasional nod, Don Saverio sat quietly, presiding over his dead son. Looking up now and then, with a washed-out smile, he greeted people milling about.

A succession of thoughts went through Ray's mind. *Is he using Stefano to show how far he would go to defend his honor? Or is he sending a message to the old Mafia with his brothers as witnesses that the game is over?*

The morticians moved Stefano's body into a shiny mahogany casket.

Ray recalled his mother words "Trust nobody," as he looked around for unfamiliar faces and then he thought about Don Saverio again. *A man of his caliber . . . in the business he is in, he has to put stuff like that behind him quickly. In fact, he couldn't have blessed Carlo unless he had written Stefano off first. But why had he turned on Stefano? As for the showing of his son, cruel as it seems, it's politics at its best—making the most of a situation.* With the ceremony of transferring the body into the casket over, Ray left for the restroom.

Still staring at his son, now in the half-open casket, after two long nods, Don Saverio rose to his feet, glanced around at all present, and said, "I would like to ask you if you could leave me alone with my son for one last time. Please."

Carlo was the last to walk out. Don Saverio approached the casket, placed his right hand on the open lid, looked down at his son, and bellowed with rage: "Bastard!" He spat on Stefano's face, slamming the casket shut. "Go to hell!"

Unaware of Don Saverio's request, Ray had returned to the room and stood quietly, out of sight, waiting for Don Saverio to return to himself. Aware of each other's presence now, both men left the room silently.

These men knew that only in the throes of such an ordeal is one forgiven for breaking the most sacred rule men of honor live by— what's in your heart should never reach your lips.

4

IN THE EARLY EVENING, Don Saverio and his two brothers sat around the dining room table. Since their father's death, this had become a routine meeting on the first Wednesday of the month.

A traitor had shot the old man during a scuffle. Before he died, he found enough strength to push his fingers through the guy's throat, tear it out, and watch him bleed to death.

With Don Saverio at the helm and Carmelo and Gaspare as counselors, the brothers vowed to defend their family at any cost. Stefano's funeral was three days old.

Leaving behind a box of cigars, a bottle of sambuca, and a pot of espresso, the wives cleared the table and retreated to do the dishes. In contrast to the men, these women had a lot to gossip about.

Gaspare filled three demitasse cups to the rim and pushed one to each brother. "How come those two kids were alone?"

"You mean Stefano and Gloria?"

"Who the hell you think I'm talking about, Carmelo? Romeo and Juliet, for God's sake?"

"Saverio, wasn't she a Campo?"

Don Saverio looked at his brothers and shook his head. "She was.

As for being alone, that's the way most people fool around. Alone—wouldn't you say, Gaspare?"

"I guess so. What pisses me off is Carmelo with his stupid questions."

Carmelo nodded, looking down at the flower pattern on the tablecloth then at his brothers. "You know, Stefano used to unload his thoughts on me. Maybe he didn't care much about traditions, but he sure wasn't that kind of a fellow. He loved Carlo. If what did him in was a rumor, that's a bad rap."

"That's a shame," said Gaspare.

Don Saverio, ready to bounce off Gaspare's stare, fiddled his cane.

"How the hell did it happen, not even a hint?" Carmelo wondered aloud.

"Look guys, I'm the one who lost a son. Let me also remind you, that I'm the head of this family. I'll take your advice when I ask for it, and I'll advise you when I think it's needed."

Don Saverio never eased off on his brothers for pulling him out of college. Back then, they claimed that, for the stability of the family, it would be best if they carried on as counselors with him taking over the old man's job. But Don Saverio knew better; neither brother wanted to give up his business. With no reproach and a pledge to reform Mafia, Don Saverio took the job.

Before college, Don Saverio was unquestioningly in favor of the way Mafia did business. In college, though, freed of constraints, he began to realize how far off course Mafia had strayed. Families were feuding over territories rather than working for the same cause their ancestors had for centuries. The ideology of Mafia was no longer the credo of men of honor. He also realized that that kind of Mafia was unacceptable to educated men.

Those years of college changed him from a would-be mobster into a man of honor with deep convictions about his heritage, a change he could not readily effect if he were to deliver on his pledge. Locked in a prison of his own making, on the surface he conducted business as usual, but at times more aggressively than his father would have. Meanwhile, in the background, his every move was planned toward a goal he considered higher than himself and his family.

He stared at his brothers. "To get off Stefano's ordeal, let me say that he wanted nothing to do with family business, nor did he honor our traditions. And that's unacceptable, especially when the rumor of him cheating on his brother was growing louder."

"Who started the rumor anyway?"

"What difference does it make, Gaspare? Even if you whack the person who started it, the rumor lives on. In fact, it'll grow faster and louder."

Don Saverio nodded. "I could've accepted him having nothing to do with family affairs, but to fight it? On the other hand, I have to hold Carlo back. Unfortunately, he just doesn't have what it takes."

"You see, Saverio? That's what concerns me. Carlo is too ambitious; don't you agree, Carmelo? He might have given you some cockamamie story, started the rumor himself, and you bought it. Maybe you were too hasty telling Carlo to take care of it. Tell me I'm wrong."

"Forget Carlo for now. Unfortunately, in our business, you have to dismiss those rumors before they start. Once they get legs, there's no telling. If I'd let Stefano's rumor grow, it would've choked us all like cancer. When the end is certain, and the ride to that end is harder than the end itself, why suffer?"

Gaspare and Carmelo nodded. "I know, rumors are no good anywhere, but I think you got duped and will never admit—"

"No, stop! Don't even think it, Gaspare. I believed Carlo. They did meet alone all summer long. To that extent, the rumor was correct, and no matter the facts, I had to act quickly for the sake of the family."

"That was your bungalow, right?"

"It is. When Stefano graduated, he wanted a place of his own. He spent most of his time there."

Gaspare grabbed a cigar. "Water under the bridge, Carmelo. . . . What's the use of talking? The man made up his mind and that's that. Saverio, on stuff like that, in the future it would be nice to let us in beforehand. We'd like to do more than just talk."

Don Saverio fixed himself another coffee and dismissed his brothers with a wave of his hand.

Carmelo was sixty-five and Gaspare sixty. In their own ways, they were men of honor with common sense and good business skills. But neither was motivated to lead the family, nor could they offer the kind of leadership the job demanded. Although Don Saverio was the youngest, neither Gaspare nor Carmelo ever failed to respect him. Their talks were candid and held in complete secrecy. No matter how intense, all feuds were over at the end of every meeting.

"What about Carlo? Is Gaspare right?"

Don Saverio put the coffee cup down. "At times, doubt can be harsher than rumor. Something tells me to watch him. Until I'm comfortable with him, he stays here with me. For now, we must be careful not to start another rumor."

"You better keep an eye on him."

"I wish my two boys were more like their sister."

"By the way, how's she?"

"I'm meeting her on Friday and Carlo tomorrow. She thinks I don't know, but she wants to talk business. On Saturday, I'm meeting Ray Greco."

"There goes your week."

"Well, that's my job. Teach them, set them in the right direction, and hope for the best."

"Are you talking about Silvana and Ray, or all of them?"

"There he goes again! Carmelo, who the hell do you think Saverio is talking about, you and me?"

"Calm down. I'm talking about the Class of '56. The time has come for them to learn what the real deal is. There can be no illusions about their role."

Carmelo scratched the palm of his hand, much as greedy people do when thinking of money. "Any news on the credit card deal? The more I think about it, the more I like it."

"With that, we must be patient. It's going to take lots of work. For now, it's right on target. The promoters know what they have. Believe me; they're on it like leeches. Give it fifteen years, tops. And like the airplane, they'll make this one fly, too. Trust me. It'll fly even higher."

Gaspare stopped puffing smoke onto the glowing tip of his cigar. "Jesus . . . fifteen years?"

"What's wrong with that? Are you going anywhere soon?"

"You mean to tell me that people won't have to use real money to buy things? You must be kidding me? In my book, money talks."

Don Saverio glanced at the two of them. "I don't have to prove a thing. Fifteen years suits me just right."

"That's right. What's the matter with you, Gaspare? Most people are emotional and impatient, like you. When they find something, they want it now. With money in their pockets to spend, if you show them what they want, they'll buy it on impulse. But without cash, the impulse fades quickly. And that's bad for business. Isn't that true, Saverio?"

"That's the idea. Likely customers always have the right emotions to make big business work. Since ancient times, through one form of credit or another, merchants sought ways to tap that market. The twentieth century has all the right ingredients. And guess what? That idea is being developed as we speak, and we want part of the action.

"They've been experimenting with it for some time. Six years ago, Diners Club and American Express launched the first charge card in America. They called it plastic money. The following year, Diners Club issued a few hundred credit cards for use in selected restaurants in New York. Wake up, Gaspare. In less than five years, the credit card is already a success."

To celebrate good things to come, Carmelo reached for a cigar and Don Saverio for the last of the espresso.

"What about Ray Greco? Does he know about his father?"

"I don't know, Carmelo. Before I turn him loose, I'll find out. But let me tell you, besides being honorable, he's the brightest and the most capable when it comes to handling our deals. There's another plus . . . I think Silvana likes him a lot."

"You're taking a big chance."

"Not in the long run. For now, I'll keep him close."

Carmelo drained his espresso, pulled out his pocket-watch, and scheduled the next dinner for Gaspare's home.

5

DON SAVERIO SPENT A GREAT DEAL OF TIME READING about the latest political and economic events. If there was anyone who complained about his reading, it was without a doubt the mailman. He had to carry the extra load halfway up Monte Bonifato. Almost every day, Don Saverio received newspapers, magazines, and books from most parts of the world. It was a large load for anyone to bear.

Don Saverio's second floor study was mission control; the large conference room, also upstairs, his battlefield. One look at his library attested that he was well read. The library was stacked with biographies of the most prominent political figures. There were also books about history, human relations, and essays on geographical and economic growth. Don Saverio and his library were an inspiration to Ray Greco.

The rustic credenza and the red maple bookcases were in harmony with the decor of the cypress-paneled studio. The chairs were handsome but, all except for Don Saverio's, were stiff and did not invite loitering. A grandfather clock stood next to the mahogany desk, and a wooden stand held a three-foot globe.

Every other day Don Saverio had to reset the clock and the globe. He was not a perfectionist, but the house cleaner never set them back.

While he thought it was a vengeful act, he took the slight with a smile to keep peace with Donna Maria.

To the right of the door was a coat hanger, and directly below it the black silvery cane and umbrella. They stood next to each other, stiff and ready.

Holding the drapes aside, Don Saverio stood at the north window looking over the city. Amid the chaotic arrangement of thousands of red-tiled roofs, he most admired the prominent churches with their centuries-old steeples, the old castle, and the middle and high schools. Alcamo Marina and Castellammare del Golfo were also in view. It intrigued him to think about how the city and its surroundings had survived centuries of conflicts, including the World War II bombings. It was through this landscape that he let his mind wander, through the hills and the valleys of the past, as he imagined the future.

As the clock struck ten, Silvana came in with a pillow under her arm. She placed it on a chair across from the desk. He waved his little girl to his side. She walked briskly to her father and clasped his hand gently. "How are you, Papa?"

He hugged her and kissed her forehead. When she showed up with a pillow, he knew she needed special attention. Although consumed by events of the funeral, she was lively as always. At twenty-three, she was the youngest of his children. Her brown eyes missed no trick. Locked in a man's world, with her every move dependent on her father's approval, she was restless. In the past, the closer she tried to get to her father, the more it set them apart.

Each time, the fact of being a woman took her back into her aunt's world of embroidering. This would only reinforce her resolve to become independent. Besides housekeeping and cooking, in Sicily, needlepoint was a vital skill for a girl to learn if she were to build a dowry that would attract a husband.

"Papa, it's been five years since I graduated from high school."

"And with honors, too, I must say."

She smiled as they walked to their seats.

"Those are moments parents can't forget."

"Papa . . . I . . . I want to go to college."

Don Saverio looked away, then glanced back at her. "College is out of town. You know how people talk around here when a single girl leaves home. You've a reputation to protect."

"But these are the fifties. Besides, I always thought you were open-minded enough to trust me."

"Silvana, listen, it's not a matter of trust. It's a matter of tradition. I know you don't like to hear that, but with us, it's a way of life. Our traditions may take several generations to catch up with the rest of the world, but that's what we live by."

"This is my generation. I simply refuse to stand by idly watching my dreams die. It's unfair. Tradition or not, I won't do it."

He never doubted she thought she knew what she wanted or why. But these were not her true desires; they were a mask for her rebellion. Being the visionary he was, he knew that unless he treated her as an adult with rights of her own, he would lose a daughter. Considering this, he was careful; for, in a peculiar way, she weighed heavily on his cause. Don Saverio sat at his desk, Silvana in her seat.

"Silvana, we all have the need to fulfill our dreams."

For the first time in their relationship, Don Saverio was biding time with what he thought was trivial talk and so he ventured on, "To fulfill our dreams doesn't mean we have to destroy what we already have. At times, dreams are better left as dreams. They often help us cope with the realities of the present."

Fascinated, she kicked her shoes off, folded her legs under her, and listened.

"But if dreams are justifiable . . . then we must definitely fulfill them."

"What do you mean . . . justifiable?"

"I don't know; it's just the way it came out. I guess when you talk from the heart things come out like that, without warning. But let me ask you, do you happen to have a justifiable dream?"

"I do!"

With a glint in her eyes, she shook her ponytail loose, walked to the window, and spelled out her plan.

"For the past few years, I've been noticing a bizarre trend in town that gave me an idea."

"And that is?"

"Take Uncle Gaspare's wine business, for example. He used to sell it in large containers: gross weight, tare, and net. No names, no labels. Now, he pours it into dark glass bottles with fancy labels. He packs twelve to a box with the buyer's name on it. Almost every other farm in the region is doing the same thing. The buyer makes money by shuffling papers. Take Uncle Carmelo's macaroni shop. He only makes a few packages with his label for the locals. The rest are packed for outsiders."

"Obviously, it's good for the economy. The locals make more money."

"I don't mind people selling their products to outsiders for more money. I agree. It's good for the local economy. What I mind are outsiders making windfall profits by draining our resources. Compared to what we could be making if we got more involved, what we're getting adds up to a fraction of its real worth."

Don Saverio nodded. She leaned on the windowsill facing him.

"There are at least a dozen other similar cases, and the number is growing across the region. Anyway, the case that concerns me most is Aunt Laura's embroidery business. She's placing American labels on my creations. Aunt Laura says I should be proud. I think it stinks. For starters, no one will ever know my name."

Her father listened.

"Day in and day out since I was seven, I've been chasing threaded needles through all sorts of fabrics. All for the sake of building a dowry for when Prince Charming shows up. Well, I've grown out of that. If my creations are good enough for others, then I'd be a fool to let them suck my blood. No. I won't allow it!"

"I understand. What's your plan?"

"I want to go to college and earn my master's in business administration. I'll work day and night to get it."

For the next two hours, he listened without dampening her enthusiasm. What amazed him was how independent her thoughts were. Her plan did not consider his wealth, nor did she express any desire for marriage, although she had spent most of her life getting ready for it. She was focused on a viable goal. She was a creator, a doer, and a leader who knew how to get things done.

"I like it! I like it very much. Let's do it!"

"Really?"

"Yes! I'll back you up. Before we put any wheels in motion though, we must lay out a plan that protects us. Then we'll start at once."

"But how, college comes first."

"You don't have to go to college; you'll do just fine. To run the business, we'll just hire brains. To market and promote your lines, we'll hire the talent from the best ad agencies. For now, let your imagination run free and keep on thinking beautiful things. Besides embroidering, look into jewelry, dresses, men's suits, leather products. Anything fashionable people buy and wear."

Her college ambition was only a stepping-stone to her future. With his backing, she could live in Rome, Milan, or New York and enter college without breaking with tradition.

"What will my job be?"

Don Saverio came around the desk. "Fashion designer, young lady . . . fashion designer."

"I like that! I like it very much, especially the young lady part."

She was leaving the room with a brighter outlook.

"Don't forget your pillow. By the way, how are things with Ray?"

"Same old story, I think he likes me."

"Is it because you're older?"

"No. It's tradition again. For now, I believe he wants lots of children and I want a career, Papa! . . . By the way, have you talked with Carlo lately? He seems depressed."

She held the doorknob waiting for an answer.

"We met yesterday. I've had better meetings with strangers."

She paused for a moment longer, then left, shutting the door behind her.

6

IN ALCAMO, A TWO O'CLOCK DINNER WAS A TRADITION. After each dinner, Don Saverio would reset his biological clock with a nap and a shower to squeeze two working days into one. Re-energized and freshly dressed, he was ready for his afternoon session.

The clock struck five as a car stopped under his window. Don Saverio could hear Ray rushing into the house and up the stairs.

Since Ray had joined Don Saverio's family, anyone who had known or talked about Ray's father was a suspect.

To avenge him with honor, Ray had to find the hit man first, who would then lead him to the man who ordered the killing and reveal the motive behind it, or implicate himself. If the motive was justifiable, then the man who ordered or did the killing was not only excused but also respected for his deed. That was a definite rule of Mafia from which he could not escape.

Schooled by Don Saverio for three years longer than his classmates, Ray trusted him implicitly. He had grown to care about Don Saverio's cause. Ray often wished that he didn't believe Don Saverio's guilt or that he could find a justifiable motive. However, every time he thought this, a curtain of shame obscured his mind. It wasn't a wish but a dilemma.

"Come in, Ray; have a seat."

"Good afternoon, Don Saverio."

Sitting in the same chair Silvana had sat in the day before, Ray thought, I always forget about these chairs.

Leaning back and rolling his fingertips against each other as he stared at Ray for a while, Don Saverio finally got down to business. "Ray, the reason I asked you here is to go over a few points before next week's general meeting."

"Don Saverio, my thoughts are yours."

Don Saverio, compelled to talk about a subject he didn't wish to, was biding his time. "Ray, let me ask you . . . what do you think of Mafia?"

"I don't think Mafia is going about it the right way. The tactics that some of these so-called Mafia people employ these days are not in keeping with the principles of our heritage. They should learn from the past and apply those experiences to the future. In a democratic society, people will give in more readily to what they perceive to be just, than simply from threats of broken legs, even if 'just' will ultimately cost their financial freedom and impose new kinds of oppression."

Ray's deliberate response did not surprise Don Saverio. What people didn't know about Ray was his hidden talent to observe and report. What set him apart was Don Saverio's teaching: first, in the art of rational reasoning by analysis of the facts and following the logic of events; second, in the art of intuition and self-control of speech and emotion; and third, in the art of decision making with full awareness of the consequences. If you asked Ray, he would promptly credit his father and grandfather's genes.

Brushing his mustache, Don Saverio stared at Ray. "Do you think I'm a Mafia man?"

"Who am I to judge? I believe you're a man dedicated to a righteous cause. In my opinion, if you succeed, generations to come will succeed as well. I look at you as the leader of a new enterprise that needs all the help it can get from the powers of your past and the strength of our future while keeping them apart. A feat only you can accomplish."

It was that kind of reasoning that Don Saverio sought in his successor. Like Ray, Don Saverio's dilemma was either to dispose of him or to bend the rules for the good of the cause. He bent the rules, but was concerned about the rumor of Ray investigating into his father's death.

They were sitting across from each other. Ray leaned forward slightly and nodded occasionally. Don Saverio watched the clouds drifting by the window. Both were biding their time for what seemed an eternity. "I hear you're digging into your father's accident."

"Not really."

"What does your mother say?"

Ray looked away. "She's not sure it was an accident. Just for her sake . . . I thought I could bring it to a close."

Since Ray had decided to investigate his father's death, he had found many flaws in the stories he had been told.

"If you feel you must get to the bottom of it, go ahead. In the process, try not to mess up your life. For what it's worth, let me assure you that back then my people looked into it and that's all it was, a freak accident."

"Please don't mistake her doubts for mine, Don Saverio."

Ray was ready to wait a lifetime to get what he wanted. For now, he was committed to trust Don Saverio and work for his cause. It was the only way to get what he wanted. Waiting silently for Don Saverio to get back on track, he thought, *if the killing was an accident, why did the hunter fade away soon after?*

To press on with his agenda, Don Saverio would look at you for a second or two then brush his mustache with the inside of his right hand before he spoke. Today was no exception.

"My own father was killed when I was twenty-two. I know how it feels. Trust me; at times life can dish out ugly deals and wreck your dreams." Don Saverio fingered his throat. "My deal was cut and dry. Quit college, come home, and run the family. And like my son now, life could hand you one of those deals, but a deal nevertheless, if you know what I mean."

"I know exactly what you mean. If you can handle the deal, that's fine. And if you can't? . . . "

"Then you're screwed!"

"Even when you're family?"

"Especially when you're family. You could waste it all for everybody."

The two men were playing Ping-Pong, using Carlo as the bouncing ball. Watching the game keenly, Ray could see Don Saverio smashing Carlo out of the game entirely.

"I don't blame you to act the way you do toward your kids. You worked hard on this new deal . . . or shall I call it 'enterprise'?"

"For now you may, but let me ask, do you think the others know about our mission?"

"Except for Victor and Angelo, they might. I'm sure they're not thinking of going abroad to convert a bunch of dysfunctional Mafia families to attending Mass on Sunday mornings, making them kiss and make up for the rest of the week as they set themselves up in fancy lifestyles of their own."

"No. I don't think so either. But then, you never know."

"Don Saverio, you know them better than I do. They're a bunch of smart fellows. They are well educated and eager to start a new life abroad."

"That they are. But, you'll see, they have quite a ways to go yet in their education."

"They might have figured that much out already. While they might dream of fancy lifestyles, they're aware of having been prepped for something other than gangsters. They are not thugs. In their own right, each is a fine would-be leader with good morals."

"Ray, how did you figure that out?"

"To me it's obvious. Although the thrust of your mission is to re-form Mafia and dismantle opposing families, I'm sure you have other people in mind for that kind of work."

"You're right. You think the others figured it out, too?"

"I don't know. But if they did, what keeps the Class of '56 so strongly bonded is most likely the secrecy of its mission."

"Although the others might have figured it out, I think we should keep it to ourselves a while longer, wouldn't you say, Ray? Just in case. Mind you, this is a big deal. By the year 2000, give or take a few years, we'll be running most political clubs and big businesses in America and in every other corner of the world, all legally. We are also making some inroads at the UN. Many suppressed nations, while food-poor are bursting with endless natural riches such as oil, minerals, and precious metals, just to mention a few."

Ray was listening earnestly.

"After we set up our people, we'll branch out. We'll allow other ethnic groups to enroll. The power this new enterprise will exert over the masses and the money it will generate for politicians and business leaders alike will influence the best of the best. That's how big this new enterprise will be."

Not knowing if "influence the best of the best" meant buy and corrupt, Ray was still fascinated by Don Saverio's account. Deep inside though, he knew that Don Saverio was nurturing something different than buying and corrupting. He just didn't know what.

"I understand your sentiment about old Mafia families' blind eye to their own self-destruction, but how and when did all this come about? What I mean is, what caused you to act?"

The light posts along the driveway were glowing. In the western sky, the setting sun was turning thin layers of clouds red.

Looking out from his chair, Don Saverio said, "Red evening sky brings good weather ahead."

Ray nodded.

Don Saverio walked to the window to admire nature's contrasting colors in the earth, sky, and autumn leaves. On the eve of a new era, he waved Ray to his side. Resting his hand on Ray's shoulder, he pointed. "Watercolors, son. That's all it takes: a good base and a few colors."

"But not everyone sees it that way."

"Precisely. What's important is that you do. That's all that matters."

He led Ray to the wet bar to celebrate their unity of thought.

Don Saverio mixed a *Cinzano*, Ray an *orzata* without liquor. With drinks in hand, they returned to their chairs. Committed to confiding in him, Don Saverio went on.

"About eleven years ago, after a grueling three-day meeting on reform with ten of the toughest families, eight from the United States and two from Canada, in that conference room, thanks to their blindness, I made up my mind. Their cowardice solidified my convictions."

As if foreseeing the future, Don Saverio paused for a short second, seemingly having second thoughts about confiding in Ray. Then he caught his breath.

"I knew then that Mafia was destined to destroy itself before the turn of the century. I could do nothing but plan against those who opposed reform. In the short period since that meeting, three of those families have wiped themselves out already."

Ray nodded.

Pulling out a yellowed newspaper clipping from a drawer, he pointed at three men sitting around smiling. A closer look revealed that the man to the right sported a large, black, bushy mustache and a sinister smile. The man in the middle, with puffy cheeks and drooping lips holding a large cigar, was staring through a pair of solid black conservative eyes that were too hard to read. The man to the left, wrapped in what looked like a military blanket, sported a half-moon smile accented by a cigarette holder pointing up as if to say, "Don't worry. Daddy is here."

The clipping was dated February 11, 1945; the headline, "Yalta Conference." The caption identified the trio as Joseph Stalin, Sir Winston Churchill, and Franklin D. Roosevelt. The small print referred to their feats and defeats and their effects on the world and the ending of all future wars.

Don Saverio waved the clipping. "Back then, this photo changed my outlook. I saw the past, the future, and where I stood. Like Mafia, communism changed from a revolution for the people to a suppressor of the people, and is therefore doomed to die.

"In a democracy, liberal and conservative alike will survive as long as everybody is happy. I could hear Roosevelt saying, 'Have I got a deal for you.' In fact, he offered two deals: the old deal and the new deal. And, as the old one failed and the new one wasn't doing too well, people paid their dues with a smile and followed him blindly."

"You mean that as long as the masses get the so-called free services and big business can skim the fat from the top, politicians will be elected and reelected under the same democratic flag just to keep the action going?"

"Exactly, Ray! That's the predictable equation. For as long as the masses seek protection and have the money to pay for it, big business will help elect sophisticated thugs, the majority of them controlled like puppets on strings.

"Look at the record. Most of the so-called democrats in America are nothing more than reformed socialists and communists or whatever other political school they come from. They will stay on until the masses are milked dry. At that point, if they want to keep going, they will have to figure out a way to replenish the masses with gullible investors and fresh taxpayers. And there are plenty of them on standby just outside the borders of the United States."

Ray realized there weren't too many people he could trust, but he also realized they often offered credible information. Mixing another *orzata*, he stroked his streak of white hair twice.

"So, Don Saverio, when we convert that equation into business terms, one can say that, for now, the first and easiest market to penetrate is the United States."

"For now, that's the case, Ray. Thanks to their inexhaustible resources, their democratic system will have the run of things for a while longer. Any governing system man devises will run aground when it has squeezed every dollar from the masses. At which time, our new enterprise will take hold and survive under any form of government the masses choose, for we'll be that government."

"In other words, your vision is to run a political Mafia?"

"No. It's to set up and run lawful businesses supported by a legal Mafia that controls all politicians like puppets on strings. After all, for the last four hundred years, Mafia has been a political force that most governments, in one way or another, have contended with. To flourish in America, Mafia needs to reform and change its identity. Let me tell you, Ray. Give the American people carefree times and relief from personal responsibility through public services such as medical care, welfare, childcare, and lots of toys like automobiles, low-cost housing, and modern gadgets—and don't forget prepared foods and disposable wares—and they'll elect and reelect anyone who promises all that good stuff, even if that good stuff slowly kills them through financial stress or debilitating diseases. Believe me, Ray; it's later than you think. The race is well underway. What's comforting, though, is that the real boom is at least twenty years away, plenty of time for us to settle in."

Wanting to hear more, Ray just watched as Don Saverio went on.

Don Saverio pointed at the bookcase. "Look what Roosevelt and his gang started with these New Deals. Thanks to them, lots of friends of mine have already made millions upon millions, and still counting."

"As you said, life can dish out a hell of a deal."

Don Saverio took another pass at his mustache. "Talking about deals, Ray, yesterday Silvana proposed a deal I think we can turn into a super-deal."

"Silvana?"

Dampening Ray's surprise, Don Saverio explained Silvana's ideas about fashion design and her desire for a career as well as his ideas on how to get things moving: such as which contractors, subcontractors, distributors, shippers, and retailers to use; and how to market and advertise new lines through worldwide contacts.

"Look, Ray. These are new times, and we can't let tradition stand in our way while the world's moving forward. She's an aggressive woman on a mission of her own. No tradition will hold her back. With or without our help, she'll move ahead, at least until she gets it out of her system."

"I didn't know she felt that way. For all I knew, she was the typical girl who longed to get married some day and raise a family. You know, I'm very fond of her. But she never said a word about this to me."

"I know, Ray. Listen carefully. For obvious reasons, I decided not to have the family name linked with any new deal. You'll be at the helm of all new deals as my *sottocapo*. Carlo will handle old business, and, with your help, Silvana will start the fashion business."

"If you want your name out of it, what about Silvana, she's a Cremona, no?"

"Not if she marries. But don't worry. The whole deal can take as long as seven years to get off the ground, as much as ten before it's fully developed. By then, you and the rest of the boys will settle down and learn how to run things. For now, let's worry about the work at hand."

Ray wasn't concerned about planning the Cremona family; he let

Don Saverio worry about that. Nor was he concerned about Don Saverio getting swindled on those new deals. More often than not, Don Saverio mulled over ideas for quite some time before he landed the right person for the job.

What concerned Ray wasn't the new enterprise nor, for a brief moment, his father's murder, but Silvana Cremona becoming Silvana Greco.

7

AFTER FIVE YEARS OF EXTRA CURRICULUM in Don Saverio's school of honor, it was the day of the much-discussed meeting. In anticipation, most classmates were speculating about their assignments. Don Saverio hooked his cane on the edge of the table, glanced at each student once, and began. It was 5 p.m. on September 21, 1956.

The setting resembled that of The Last Supper, except the Master, Don Saverio, was facing his disciples. Across and to his right were Angelo Sutera and four others; to his left were Victor Como and four others. Facing each other at the opposite ends of the table were Carlo and Ray.

The vaulted ceiling, trimmed with a Florentine border, matched the delicate gold, green, and blue shade of the walls; by design, there were no windows. The three crystal chandeliers that hung directly above the long table illuminated the large conference room. A Persian rug covered the marble floor. There were small trays of refreshments for each seat. Three bottles of red wine and three baskets of fresh fruit were clustered on the table below each chandelier, creating a friendly, if not cozy, atmosphere.

The door was closed and the entire second floor kept off-limits to outsiders, even though Don Saverio's most trusted men stood guard indoors and out. These men were proficient at what they did. Secret meetings were almost weekly occurrences at the villa.

"Gentlemen, I'll get right to the point. Our mission is to infiltrate the United States political system and big business from within. This feat I estimate will take the better part of the next ten years . . . just to get it up and running. When I say from within, I mean from the grass roots of the American political system. The colleges and universities where Americans first form and nurture their political clubs.

"In these clubs, you will mingle with the rich and powerful and the upcoming candidates for political stardom. From there you will enter the political arena and the corporations, paving the road for those who will follow in your footsteps. That includes people from other ethnic groups and American generations to come.

"The number of groups making up our people will be large enough to fill both houses of Congress to overflowing. This move will reform the largest political club of them all."

"The man is insane," whispered one classmate to another at the far end of the table, as the others reached for water to help disguise their astonishment.

Their apparent concern did not perturb Don Saverio. "To break from within, we must first set up bases in some of their most populous and richest states, New York, New Jersey, Illinois, Connecticut, Massachusetts, California, and Texas, then target their most prestigious universities in the northeastern region.

"Your residences and your designated campus grounds will give you a dual base from which to work. In order to be accepted by your new communities, before you apply to any universities, you'll spend two years at the most prominent prep schools. There you will strive for the highest academic grades and learn how to speak like an American. In so doing, you will also build good fellowship credentials and gain popularity by joining social, athletic, and community events."

Alarmed by the idea of two years of prep school, most of them thought, God knows how much more he wants us to slave on books. For a short moment, they looked away. Then, respecting the man they had come to admire over the years, they paid attention to the speech.

"Later on, when you enter college, I see no reason for you not to become the most sought-after students by fraternity houses and other prominent groups, on and off campus. When that happens, you'll know you have arrived. Can anyone say it wouldn't be so?"

He swept his gaze to the right and to the left and, sensing tension, he toned down his speech. "In time, your hard work, coupled with your extra-good looks, like Victor here, will give you the run of the town."

Except for Victor, no one smiled or relaxed. They were young, too serious about themselves, and too tense about their futures. They were worried about the two further years of school, not to mention college. They could easily accept college, but prep school? *Please*, they thought.

If they thought that Don Saverio would arrange for their college admission, they had missed the boat entirely. Nothing illegal, Ray thought, staring at Carlo.

"Look, guys, nothing would please me more than to see you out of college four years from now. But that would just get you out of college fast and see you drop out of sight even faster. There is too much at stake here to rush things. The world you're about to enter is the big league, where stakes are high and mediocrity is not accepted. In fact, when you get good at what you do, don't stop there; get better. When you get bright and smart, everyone will be after you, pulling you to their side, ready to do whatever you ask of them."

He scanned each face once more. "To be effective, though, you must earn each and every credit on your own, fair and square. Prep school will help you achieve that with ease. Besides, where else can you mingle with most of your future college classmates?

"For the success of our mission, I can't stress anything more important than this. Just be yourselves, relax a little, and apply all you have learned with me. Above all, have fun doing it. I'll guarantee that before you know it, you'll be out of school as one of them—rich and powerful—and because you are already rich, you might say the job is half done.

"Just remember: planning, perseverance, and hard work will always produce large dividends. Like my father used to say, it only takes one match to start a big fire."

"Don Saverio, I believe they would like to know their final roles."

They all seconded Ray with a nod.

"Let me put you at ease. None of you will need to run for elected office. To help mold the newly elected, we need you at your jobs for more than a term or two. Your job is to influence and guide them in what we think they should be, men of honor with backbones."

"I'll accept your theory, but how?"

"Good question, Angelo. Always remember that the people in the background carry the heaviest load. In other words, behind every successful leader, there is a staffer or two and more speechwriters, strategists, consultants. The more you stay in the background, trading punches with friends and foes, the better you get at what you do and the more indispensable you'll be. The rest is easy. On its own, our ideology will spread like wildfire, infiltrating politics and big business from within."

"Don Saverio, we want you to know that we're committed to your cause. We truly appreciate your trust, and you can count on us."

"Thank you, Marco. At one time I was young and in college, too. You'll do just fine. Just remember, by the time you get out of college, your input will help Ray lay out a road map to the most vulnerable posts for you to attack."

Across the table, there were now smiles of admiration and acceptance.

Most members of the Class of '56 would be able to enter the United States permanently. For the rest, it was student visas. To be assigned student status, each member had to set up a trust account in America then prepay part of the tuition and pay for room and board with people not linked to Mafia.

Don Saverio had waited ten years for this moment. During that time, he had laid out every detail summed up in three never-to-be-broken rules:

Never break American laws.
Never associate with members of the old Mafia.
Never take on money or women problems.

"In America, Ray will be your liaison. He will be the only link between you and me. When you communicate among yourselves, be discreet. Always assume that someone is listening. Remember the old cliché: walls have eyes and ears. Technology is getting better by the day. Be cautious when writing documents or notes. They tend to show up when they are least convenient. They can destroy grand careers. Keep all your fiscal and private records in order and ready for magnifying-glass scrutiny. One false step and you will be out of the game and no one will come to your aid."

To stress his next point, Don Saverio looked at Ray. "Fourteen months from now, on November 14, 1957, in Appalachia, New York, sixty heads of Mafia families, in an attempt to reorganize, will attend the largest meeting of its kind ever assembled. I declined the invitation for it can be trouble for us. Make a mental note of that date. Stay clear of the area, and be aware of anything you say, especially when you recognize some of the people involved. The media will have a field day. It only takes a single unwary answer to make worldwide headlines. This event will be the first to give you a firsthand taste of prejudice. America is full of it. If you're not alert, you'll fall for its fallacies and regress instead of progress in your mission.

"Because we're Sicilians, people will always associate us with Mafia. This can be detrimental or beneficial to you. It'll depend on how you handle the situation. Ironically, if you take the obvious action and distance yourself from Mafia, you'll have the most advantage. No matter what you say or do, the doubt will always linger in most people's minds; so will their respect for your words and actions. For example, next time such an event grabs the headlines, you'll find the same people, in a subtle kind of way, asking the same questions just to test your integrity. As a precaution, you'll find that a few derogatory comments about Mafia will always bring you a step closer to your objective. That is, being accepted as one of them."

The Class of '56, having accepted all his conditions, was puzzled at the mention of prejudice. It was nonexistent in Sicily. Wisely, Don Saverio called for a break.

Carlo called the meeting back to order.

"With my father's permission . . . I would like to propose a vote of confidence for Ray."

Don Saverio waved Carlo on.

"With Ray at the helm of the new enterprises, I think it is vital that we take a vote showing our support for the difficult job he's undertaking."

Victor seconded the motion, raising his hand, as did Angelo, Ralph, Marco, Michael, Joseph, John, Tony, Paul, and Luca. To reinforce their solidarity, Don Saverio raised his glass to propose a toast that concluded with a round of applause.

Sporting his contagious smile, Ray accepted the vote with gratitude.

"Until things get on track, you will not be alone. Our good friends in America will be watching, ready to assist you. Those are our people reporting to me."

Marco leaned toward Ray. "I don't know what he's driving at, but I think he's pumping himself up for nothing. His days are numbered."

Ray looked the other way as Carlo continued. "They were told not to interfere unless they need to identify themselves; you probably will not recognize any of them. If you do, make no contact. Talk to no one but Ray; he'll know what to do. For the future, I'd like to show you the draft of an insignia I'm working on so you can recognize worthy associates."

The artist's rendition showed a diamond-shaped object with a blue surface on which a small shiny star streaked through a classically scripted letter A. The year 1956 was written in a stone-like font. The insignia looked like a coin without a border.

Angelo, pointing at the insignia, looked at Victor. "Powerful . . . look what I just noticed. The letter 'A' not only stands for Alcamo but for August as well. Maybe if I keep pushing, it'll stand for Angelo or maybe America, too."

With drinks in hand, they joined Angelo in much-needed laughter. Carlo called the meeting back to order.

"In the future, you might see this insignia on rings, lapel pins, paper stickers, and any other form that will help identify our people.

"Don't forget, though, the insignia will only identify its bearer as a friend or mark a transaction worth looking into. Beyond that, you must always get clearance from Ray before you engage in any dealings with others."

The Class of '56 was elated by the choice, as it made them all feel reassured and better anchored to the cause.

Ray sipped some water and pulled on his red suspenders. "Harvard, Princeton, Cornell, Yale, Georgetown, Stanford, and a few others are the universities we target for now. As much as I would love to, I will not attend college. While you're in school, Silvana and I will start a fashion business. With the help of good friends, I'm sure that by the time you're out of school, it will have turned into a big business."

Skeptical as they were about Silvana, just as Ray had been earlier in the week, the Class of '56 paid keen attention. He told them how the post-war period affected the new generation, with their insatiable desire to imitate Hollywood fashion. He explained how it was all related to marketing fashionable products worldwide. He also explained the inner workings of the new business and Don Saverio's relations with a network of contractors and marketing people. Above all, he explained how talented and committed Silvana was to developing the business.

"By the way," cut in Don Saverio with a smile, "she asked me to tell you to be on the lookout for a new fashion label, Giglio, you know, lily. She thought of it last night."

Ray turned back to the Class of '56. "I wish you luck. I'll see you on the other side. I always wanted to see the other side of the water, anyway."

Don Saverio took the floor once more. "Before we adjourn, I want to talk about our mission and the reason we must set up shop in America. All legally, mind you. In a free society, the amount of money one controls is equal to the amount of power one can exert."

They all agreed.

"To draw in the young and educated people, we must dismantle old Mafia. This has to be done as we infiltrate politics and big business."

He paused. His tone was dramatic now.

"Today, Mafia violates every rule of decency laid down centuries ago by our ancestors. While living under totalitarian governments, they adopted a code of secrecy for the survival of their cause. It was later known as *omertà*. The code, coupled with fair and swift justice, gave the victim's family instant respect. It instilled pride and confidence in every member. As an independent revolutionary body, Mafia sheltered its people from oppression. Their strategy, like ours now, was effective. Spread across the countryside in as many independent groups as possible then infiltrate the ruling government, the aim being to expand and unify to strengthen the cause. Contrary to historians' accounts, our ancestors were no criminals. Taking into account the ruthless suppression they endured, we should never forget their relentless drive for self-rule. Many societies became extinct by yielding to the will of their oppressors. Our ancestors got their resources from their oppressors any way they could. To defend their own, Mafia leaders were no less daring than any man of political principles today. As late as 1948, they rendered Sicily independent from the Italian government. Today, regardless of geopolitical maps and understanding, Sicily is autonomous, with its own council. The assembly consists of counselors and a president who's popularly elected. Sicilians, thanks to Mafia, elect their own government, not outsiders."

Don Saverio stood more erect now.

"I'm proud of my heritage.

"The Mafia I know, not gangsters, has been instrumental in scores of government reforms over the years. Mafia enhanced our way of life and increased our people's acceptance worldwide. Your level of education and of those who will emigrate after you is the living proof of those reforms. Your blood is tinted with the same talent as that of our ancestors. I will not allow any of our future generations to waste their talents on a decaying institution on its way to self-destruction. And I'm talking about the present Mafia.

"Our cause, like that of our ancestors, is a cause filled with honor, pride, and self-respect. We have to protect our heritage at any cost. The current Mafia, with no concern for their heritage, is congregating in small tribes, distrustful and ready to kill each other at the turn of a coin. Their passion for killing each other is an act of greed and suppression that lacks logic and purpose. Some of these families have strayed off course far beyond recovery. They are leaving a stigma on an entire population.

"When faced with family feuds over rank or territory, they kill each other rather than trying to reconcile and unify. They defeat the very principle of *omertà* they claim to live by. They seek media coverage to advance their power within their limited tribes. For as long as none of his people helps to put him away for life, the survivor declares himself a self-made leader. At no time has Mafia ever been faced with such a spectacle."

Don Saverio held everyone's attention. "In an open society, today's Mafia is a stigma. It stands out like a sore thumb. They deal in prostitution, drugs, gambling, loan sharking, and any other illegal activity they can mastermind. Some might even get to be glamorous enough to attract attention, but with no good values. Contrary to our values, they are criminals with a vision obscured by greed.

"Because the power of this self-proclaimed Mafia stems from the terrorizing and suppression of similar thugs, we shall do all we can to put them out of business, or at least distance ourselves as much as possible.

"In fairness to the men of honor out there who will join those already serving our cause, I ask you to respect them when they cross your path. They are an intrinsic part of our mission. Whenever necessary, they will identify themselves displaying the Class of '56 symbol Carlo just showed you.

"As you know, next week there will be a dinner honoring all the 1956 graduates in Alcamo. There you'll meet the men committed to our cause. They'll keep on working with Carlo and me. They will also migrate to the United States before the end of the year. Their mission, unlike yours, is to infiltrate old Mafia from within."

After the meeting adjourned, a strange thing happened. Ten young men's dreams of reforming a bunch of Mafia families as they set themselves up in lives of luxury became one unified dream, with the sole purpose of advancing their ancestors' ideology. For that, they committed themselves to follow Ray's lead; for without a leader and a set of rigid rules, their dream would die.

8

AFTER WORLD WAR II, nothing else molded people into the modern lifestyle more than movie theaters and dance halls. Alcamo was blessed with two of those locales: Cinema Esperia at the east end of town and Sala Arlecchino at the west end. In the ballroom, people sported fashions and espoused the liberal ideas they had learned from the movies. Changes were certainly taking hold, but because it was all new, not too swiftly.

Cinema Esperia's spacious ground floor and horseshoe mezzanine was in keeping with its wide screen, the stereo sound, and the new films it featured. The comfortable chairs made movie-going a special experience. Thanks to a mirrored wall, the lobby looked twice as deep as it really was. It wasn't until the word spread through town about this wall that moviegoers stopped slamming into it as they attempted to walk through it. After all, mirrored walls, like new fashion designs, were yet to become part of their imagination, much less reality.

Celebrations in the modern dance hall marked the start of an era in which the young defied the old. Prior to these changing times, dance halls had been primarily used for wedding receptions, and there was as always a *bastoniere*, a chief chaperon. Now, a young man no longer needed permission from the *bastoniere* to dance with the girl of his liking. In this ballroom, there was no *bastoniere*. A young man, if he could survive the hostile gaze of most parents, could invite a girl to dance from afar with a single bow of the head. More shocking, though, was the girl's newfound right to refuse.

"The *bastoniere* is a thing of the past."

"The *bastoniere* knows who's who, and who but the *bastoniere* can split a couple dancing too closely?"

"Times have changed indeed."

Unlike the older halls that held only a few rows of chairs around the dance floor, Sala Arlecchino was large enough to hold forty tables for ten. Each table held a flower arrangement and a couple of bottles of refreshments. If patrons were dining, the table could also hold a complete serving including dishes, silverware, glasses, napkins, and toothpicks.

Scotch, once a taboo, was replacing ice cream and soda, again thanks to the macho characters in the movies. The movies also showed the serving of two- and three-course dinners in public, an event previously unheard of. Dining out had been thought a sin, even if it were affordable. Before these times, the most one could get at these gatherings was a sliver of the wedding cake and a glass of wine.

Then there was champagne. While it was considered an elegant touch, few had acquired a taste for it, so often it was left to bubble itself away. Again, that was when dance halls were used mostly for weddings and chaperons were hired to keep the young in check.

The gathering was in keeping with the times. Perhaps it was Don Saverio's vision that allowed these changes to take place. Perhaps it was just the times. Perhaps it was a little of both. Anyhow, the mixture was just right. Tonight wasn't the time to talk about changing times. The celebration belonged not only to the Class of '56, but to all those graduating in Alcamo that year.

Sala Arlecchino was the place where the men of honor had come to celebrate their cause, Mafia reform. The hall was illuminated by an array of different colored fluorescent lamps nestled in coves that spanned the ceiling from wall to wall. Despite this, the designer failed to create the rainbow effect and the cozy feeling dancers had come to expect. Regardless of the atmosphere the lighting scheme evoked, like the mirrored walls, fluorescent lamps were too modern as well.

To the right side of the hall, away from the loudspeakers, Carlo was discovering scotch and soda as he waited for his parents to arrive. A table had been reserved for his family. At the opposite side of the hall, there was a table for two for Ray. Out of respect for her dead husband, however, Ray's mother did not attend the party. The Class of '56 and Don Saverio's other protégés and their families were accommodated at other tables. Two nationally acclaimed bands had come from Rome for the young. To soothe the older crowd, there was a piano player and a singer.

Contrary to local tradition, Victor was the first to ever take a girl on a date alone without ruining her reputation. To the astonishment of his family and the entire hall, Victor walked through the main entrance arm-in-arm with Brigitte to a table next to Ray's. Other novelties were Brigitte's soft ash-blonde hair and the fact that she was one inch taller than he was.

No chaperon from the girl's family was there to look over their shoulders. With her mother's blessing, Victor had broken the rules. Mrs. Stabile herself had asked Victor to take Brigitte to the party. She and her daughter were visiting from Tunisia. The mother was determined to find a date for her daughter to remember before they went back home where dating without a chaperon was strictly prohibited.

Escorting Silvana, Ray entered after Victor. Ray was dressed in a black suit with cuffless trousers, another first, sporting a million dollar smile and a Superman physique.

Like a fashion model, Silvana led the way. She walked in perfect cadence, wearing the simplest and most elegant black-sequin dress ever seen on a young woman. She wore a white lily, a *giglio*, on her left shoulder and a French-twist hairdo. The short-sleeved dress reached just below her knees, also another first. A golden hand-purse matched the gold necklace that accented the dress' scoop neckline. A pair of black high-heeled shoes and shadow-black seamless nylon stockings complemented the flattering dress. Each step she took revealed her sensuous bodyline.

A closer look revealed the details of her creation. Each of the hundreds of sequins was placed precisely in the center of small diamond-like satin embroidery that made the dress sparkle even more. The dress was the first of Giglio Enterprises' fashion line.

Consumed by the experience and the gaze of the onlookers, their body temperature rose even more when they sat at their table. Ray and Silvana stared at each other in silence, trying to figure out what to do next. After a moment, they glanced at Victor and Brigitte but got no hint. They looked around for any cue. Then, as though in answer to a prayer, the band played, "Love Is a Many-Splendored Thing." The foursome was the first to dance for the night. By the second refrain, they danced almost unnoticed on the crowded floor.

By the time his parents arrived, Carlo was half-drunk. Unaware of the squeeze Ray and Silvana were in, Don Saverio nodded and the band played on.

At the end of that first song, Carlo was admiring his mother's subtle smile as she looked at Ray and Silvana across the hall. They were enjoying their first talk alone. Carlo realized that changes had hit home, too. He also realized that his mother wasn't powerless after all. In a peculiar way, she had exerted her will on Don Saverio to let Silvana and Ray date by themselves.

It wasn't until well into the night that Silvana and Ray walked over to her parents' table. No sooner did she hear her daughter say "Powder room . . ." than Donna Maria was on her way with Silvana in tow, leaving the three men to themselves.

"Well done, Carlo. I saw a dozen people wearing our insignia already."

"Ray, with plenty of overtime, the jeweler got them ready in time. By the way, how do they look?"

"They're sharp." Ray discounted Carlo's presence and looked at Don Saverio "Do you think they'll do the job?"

"They'll do the job." He pushed the table's flower arrangement to one side and lowered his voice. "In our business, to know is always better than to be known. In your own words, Ray, 'Our mission is to strengthen through the powers of our past and yet keep the past from overshadowing the future.'

"Ray, take a good look at them here. They're the grunts of our mission. With the support of our people abroad, they'll be working the front lines. In time, they'll place themselves with families of our choosing.

"Before you leave, Carlo will give you their identities and whereabouts."

Not too sure of what was said, Carlo garbled, "Oh, sure."

With great hopes for the future, Ray and Silvana returned to their table. They were looking at each other in wonder. In their hearts, each knew what the future held, but neither spoke about it. Silvana wanted freedom from the old traditions; Ray wanted to discover the motive behind his father's killing.

Both wanted to go on with their lives. Stubbornly, each thought they knew the other better. Stubbornly, if it were not for this time together, they would have parted without ever knowing each other at all.

"I hear you're going by sea."

"That's right."

"Why?"

"After my friend's tale of his trip from New York last month, I simply refuse to fly for now."

"What happened?"

"The only thing he could see that night was flames coming out of the engines and propellers spinning almost red. I'll wait for the jet before I think of flying. It will be in service soon."

"You're not choosing the ocean liner because of its nightclubs, are you?" Feeling a sudden pang of jealousy, she smoothed things over with a passionate smile.

"Silvana, what do you really want out of life?"

"I want to be an independent human being, valued for who I am and what I do. Only then will I be ready to set up house and raise a family."

He said nothing, but rubbed his streak of white hair twice.

Her passion for business made her sound more like an entrepreneur than the romantic person she really was. Because he sensed her fervent passion, he worked her carefully, as if taming a wild mare. Not for the prize, but for the love she could offer.

"And what do you want?"

Hesitant, faced with the dilemma of choosing between the cost of what the outcome of their conversation could be and the need to know whether she was ready to part from her father, he chose the possible cost. Ray cradled the glass in both hands.

"With one exception, the same things you do. But before I settle down, I must comfort my mother and myself. I have to discover the motive behind my father's killing. I must put that behind me. My mother and I need to move on."

"Why the motive?"

"I think I know who ordered the killing. I only hope the motive was justifiable."

"And if it is?"

He whirled the ice cubes around with his finger. "If the killing was justifiable, no matter how close to the killer or to the victim you are, as a man of honor you must accept the event without prejudice. Throughout history, many men of honor sentenced their own when they found them guilty—do you subscribe to that?"

She took his hand in hers. "It's the only rule of justice I know. If I might add, no matter how much it hurts, you must always accept its outcome."

"You mean like Stefano's and Gloria's?"

"Truthfully, Ray, I'm having second thoughts about the ordeal, but it's too late to do anything. And as much as I feel for her, she wasn't family."

"I knew her well. She came from a proud family. For the life of me, I can't imagine her cheating, especially with Stefano. Again, life gets complicated at times."

"I'm too remote to feel their pain, or, for that matter, even yours. I'm sure that if there was foul play in either case, the truth will come out. And when it does, I must accept it, even if it involves my family."

Watching Victor and Brigitte on the dance floor, Ray and Silvana started their relationship not with small talk over a glass of greenish punch, but with honesty and respect for each other's convictions. And so they danced the night away.

9

IT WAS THE DAY BEFORE RAY LEFT FOR AMERICA, and he had yet to visit his father's grave. Since his father's death fourteen years earlier, he had only visited twice. Not out of lack of love or respect, but due to the cold relationship between the Grecos and his mother.

That afternoon, riding along Corso 6 Aprile, Alcamo's thoroughfare, he found himself turning north, then down a dirt road and curving toward the right to the old water fountain. He drove a short way and stopped at the first cemetery. Alcamo's two cemeteries were known as the First and Second Cemeteries. The first was the older of the two.

Strolling through an array of headstones, he reached the mausoleum that was his father's resting place. On his way, he read most of the epitaphs, saluting the deceased as if they were old friends. The lifelike photos on the headstones made them seem alive. At the end, under the autumn foliage, he climbed six steps. A few feet to the right was his father's tablet.

Since his last visit, Ray had grown taller, and he no longer had to stand on tiptoe for a glimpse of the photo. At eye level now, he found his father much younger than he remembered. The engraving read:

LUCIANO GRECO
JUNE 18, 1914 – OCTOBER 12, 1942
LUCIANO NOW LIVES THROUGH HIS SON, RAY

The writing meant something more than a scribble. With tears blurring his vision, Ray vowed, "I'll get them, Dad. I promise, I will."

Leaning forward with both his palms pressing on the upper corners of the tablet, Ray read the script over and over again.

A footstep echoed off the floor behind him. From the corner of his eye, he saw the shadow of a man. Frozen in thought, he stood still. When the man touched his shoulder, he swung around only to find himself wrapped in the man's arms. "Grandpa, I'll get them . . . I'll get them."

The deep-voiced man said, "I know you will. I know you will, son."

Grandpa and Ray were strolling along the arched veranda that stretched alongside the mausoleum overlooking the cemetery. The trees had ceased to cast long shadows. In the red twilight, each step echoed off the marble wall in sync with the words they spoke and the hooting of the owls.

The old man rested his hand on Ray's shoulder. "It feels good. I waited a long time for this moment."

At seventy-five, Grandpa was as tall as Ray. He wore a large brown hat with a small pheasant's feather on the right. His black cape reached just below his knees. His well-polished knee-high boots gave him the look of a well-to-do farmer.

"Grandpa . . . I don't know what to say. Sometimes life can be unfair. Tomorrow I'm leaving for—"

"You don't have to explain, young man. I know all about it. Lately, I've been talking with your mother. I can only say I should have done it sooner. As you said, sometimes life can be unfair. And just for being stubborn, we often pay a price."

"I'm glad you're talking with her now."

He faced Ray squarely. "She's a good woman. She has raised a fine man. Tradition or not, before you get to America, I'll have the entire family talking. She'll have a family to count on."

"As to my father, before I make a move, I must know who pulled the trigger and why."

"I've followed your every move since you joined the Cremonas. As much as I've promised not to interfere and as much as it kills me, deep inside I know that only by staying close to them will you learn the facts and stay true to your calling."

"Perhaps my way of doing things is different. I'm not saying my father did something wrong. I want to avenge him with honor."

"Son, you said it right. That's the way it has to be, no matter how long it takes. That is *omertà*. When you get to America, look for a man named Santo Pellegrino. He's not from Alcamo. He's slick, moves around a lot, and rumor has it that some families there protect him. Some say he's their best hit man. When you find him, he'll most likely give you all sorts of stories. They say he's afraid of nothing, but I don't buy that. I think he's a coward. He left shortly after your father was killed. He's missing his left forefinger. The last I heard, he was in Brooklyn. Talk with Sal Rocca."

"I have."

"Sal appreciates the job you gave him. He's very loyal to our family. He's ready to help you with whatever it takes. Remember, he wants to avenge your father more than we'll ever know."

"I know that. My father trusted him implicitly. And do you know what I remember most about Sal?"

Grandpa smiled.

"When I was a kid, he always gave me a wooden soldier whenever Dad and I visited him at the job sites."

Grandpa smiled again, but said nothing.

Ray was as excited as a kid. "And guess what? I got one every Christmas until last."

Grandpa reached in his pocket, "You mean just like this one?"

Ray paused and with glinting eyes he stared at the old man and smiled. Instantly, he knew that the hands that carved the one in his grandfather's hand had also carved the others in his collection.

As they parted, Ray shook his head, watching as the darkness of the night enveloped Grandpa.

10

IN BROOKLYN, THE WINTER OF '56 saw the most snow ever. Except for one short morning back in Alcamo, this was Ray's first experience with snowstorms.

His legs still wobbly from eleven days spent at sea, Ray rented a two-story apartment in a three-family house on Harman Street. With dark-brown shingles and a waist-high black-iron fence, the house resembled a brownstone of some sort. The fence enclosed the front yard but not the stoop. Through a gate to the right of the stoop, clear of two trashcans, a walkway led to the ground floor entrance. This floor included the kitchen, dining, and laundry rooms. In the dining room, a spiral staircase wound up to the living room. The setup gave the living room a theatrical atmosphere. The upstairs quarters were also accessible from the first floor main entrance. Except for when he put out the trash, Ray hardly ever used the ground floor entrance. He would climb up the stoop and check the mail first, then take three steps down the hall and disappear into his apartment. Once inside, the spiral staircase almost forced him downstairs. If he missed the door and kept on walking down the hall and up a flight of stairs, he'd face a fire escape ladder leading up to the roof through a hatchway. There was no lock there. People could come down from the roof at will.

On Harman Street, Ray learned all about snow removal, tire chains, alternate street parking, city buses, elevated trains, and subway routes. The never-ending lines of parked cars on both sides of the street captivated Ray. With few parking spaces up for grabs, he tried to avoid the city's tow truck by parking on the lawful side the night before. If he couldn't find a legal spot, he would get up early next morning and maybe find one.

This morning, Ray came out of the vestibule and onto the stoop. With not a single car in sight, he stretched his neck out for a better view. Then, taking one more step forward, he tumbled down the stoop, engulfing himself in snow up to his ears. He laughed his heart out at his blunder.

It seemed as though all the snow that had fallen overnight in Brooklyn had piled up on Harman Street. Cars, stoops, railings, garbage cans, basement windows, front yards, and everything that make up a city street were covered in snow. Only the main entrances above street level could be seen. The snow-covered street looked like a barren open field sprinkled with shiny twigs, the radio antennas from buried cars below.

Seven days later, Ray dug his car out. However, it was a losing proposition. Every freezing day after the storm, the city plow piled up more snow on the parked cars. The locals thought it was a conspiracy to keep them off the roads. Since Ray didn't mind public transportation, the conspiracy was fine with him. A short walk to the Wilson Avenue bus stop and fifteen cents took him anywhere in the city he wanted to go and kept him warm to boot.

Ray was eager to start working on Don Saverio's new enterprise, a task that would allow him to seek out Santo Pellegrino before the boys graduated and he married Silvana and joined Giglio full time. With that goal in mind, he set up communication channels with each of the boys across the country first. Then he began to mingle with the locals of Bushwick.

He had chosen this area for its rich mix of Italian descendants. Another plus was that no single Mafia family dominated the neighborhood. Members of different families were there, but they worked and lived in harmony and away from their working territories, the other neighborhoods.

Unlike social clubs, the Starr Street poolroom, off Knickerbocker Avenue, was the place for criminals and hustlers to mingle with church-goers and other nice people. A newcomer could learn the makeup of the neighborhood and its scheduled and unscheduled events the media didn't report. In short, it was open to people from all walks of life. No membership fee was required, just enough cash to pay for games and lost bets.

The tables captivated Ray. Each had a hooded fluorescent fixture over the green felt waiting for the players to turn on and break a game. Looking at the table next to him, imagining the break, Ray could hear the blast followed by the thump of a ball dropping.

Two cue racks, six wooden benches, and two vending machines for cigarettes and sodas decorated the walls. The owner, a thin, middle-aged man, received and dispatched messages better than an answering machine could. In that same fashion, he tracked down monies due him plus interest. The 1½ percent weekly interest he charged was a bargain compared to the going 3 percent rate. Amazingly, the thin man subdued scuffles that would otherwise have erupted into violent fights. He was a bundle of nerves with lots of contacts. He could have had anyone's legs broken without lifting a finger. No fighting was allowed in his poolroom, although there were plenty of memories of bloodshed among the patrons.

Here, Ray met many faceless people, quickly improving his perception about the good, the bad, and the in-between fellows and the hustlers; where they came from and where they were headed; without ever stroking his white streak of hair, except when he dealt with non-Italians. Ray had never been exposed to such a diversity of races.

The Starr Street poolroom and social clubs in Bushwick were his starting point for seeking out Santo. This Friday night folks were late in arriving. A nondescript man stepped down onto the poolroom floor. Ray was playing with a cue ball at an unlit table.

Grabbing a cue stick from the rack, the faceless man approached Ray, "How you doing?"

Ray bounced the cue ball off the side cushion, "Fine."

The faceless man rolled the cue stick on the table watching it keenly, and then asked, "Did you get paid? Want to shoot some pool?"

Ray narrowed his eyes. "Get paid for what?"

"You got no job, do you?"

"What's it to you? . . . And take that stick off the table before I shove it up—"

Before Ray could finish his sentence, the faceless man grabbed a cue stick, planted the butt of it to his left shoulder, like a sharpshooter, and aimed in at the far wall, checking its line. Unhappy with it, he tried another stick. He smirked.

"Let me tell you. . . . If you got cash, whether you have a job or not means shit to me."

"I got cash. . . . But no thanks."

"You've got no job, do you?"

"What's it to you?"

"I told you already. I don't care much about a job myself."

Ray stared at him for a long moment.

The faceless man sized up Ray's massive neck and wrists cautiously. "I take it you just got off the boat, didn't you? I tell you this for your own good, get a job. Any job, at least until the word spreads, or people will stop talking to you, and soon you'll be labeled a loser."

Ray kept staring.

The faceless man bounced the cue stick back into the rack. "There's no action here. Lots of luck . . . I have to go. By the way, I like your red suspenders, but do something about that bit of white hair, I know better."

Ray watched him climb the two steps and leave.

In Bushwick, each Sicilian club-goer belonged to his own social club with a hierarchy that tied him to his community back in Sicily. It was a scheme that would help Ray search out Santo. His immediate concern, however, wasn't how to find Santo—he sensed he was in the right neighborhood—but how to make him tell the truth before he disposed of him.

"How are you?" "When did you get here?" "What you do for a living?" "Are you working?" "How is your mother? Is she coming soon?" That litany of questions from friends, relatives, and new and old acquaintances followed by subtle frowns prompted Ray to look for a job, any job, quickly. His idle presence in the neighborhood during working hours was noticeable. He found that empty greetings and chats about the weather didn't do the job. The faceless man was right. Ray got himself a job, but he did nothing about his hair. No sooner did the word spread, than a friend of a friend invited him to dinner.

Mr. Catania lived on Troutman Street, a block away from the pool-room. Alerted by a matchmaker, Mr. Catania had set eyes on Ray for his Concetta. Ray was pleased by the invitation. The spaghetti, meatballs, and veal cutlets tasted almost as good as his mother's. To show off Concetta, Mrs. Catania asked her to clear the table and serve coffee. With coffee duly served, the hollow-eyed and ready-to-smile Concetta sat across from Ray. Mrs. Catania complemented the coffee with a basket of walnuts and a tray of cookies. Mr. Catania made a mess while waiting for the coffee to cool. He pounded three walnuts with his bare hand, spreading them across the table. Then he picked at and munched the nut crumbs like a rabbit. "My friend tells me you work in the city."

Often, Ray had to stretch the truth to fit the moment. "Yes, I'm a bookkeeper, but for now I work as a labor recruiter for a dressmaker in Manhattan."

Mr. Catania rubbed his full belly. "That's good. A man over eighteen has to be a man with a trade; for that matter, a girl too has to have a steady job. Concetta is a beautician with a steady income. And a good one too, I might say."

Concetta blushed and smiled, but said nothing.

Ray cracked a walnut for Concetta and one for himself, covering the nutcracker with his hand. "Yes, you got it right. In Sicily, those are the rules."

The locals of Bushwick were vital to Ray's pursuit of Santo. To that end, he dined with many different people.

In Brooklyn, Ray learned why Don Saverio and Carlo shipped their most-trusted men into large tenements in quieter neighborhoods. South Brooklyn and parts of Queens offered the largest selections of those kinds of buildings. There, the neighbors asked no questions as long as they were asked none themselves. In effect, Manhattan, Staten Island, and the Bronx were out of reach, giving Ray more room to work. At his job, Ray gained firsthand experience of the garment business. Most significantly, though, the job gave him much-needed social status in Bushwick.

To quiz Ray, Mr. Catania improvised a dialogue. "Isn't your boss mister . . . what's his name?" he snapped his fingers a few times and winked at his wife.

"You know, the guy that makes the headline all the time . . . what's his name?"

"Mr. Catania, believe it or not, I never met the man. Nor do I know his name. The only thing I care about is my paycheck on Friday."

Concetta mirrored Ray's smile, served more coffee, and said nothing. Her father was on a roll, and she stood no chance of entering the conversation. Nor did Ray ask her questions.

Mr. Catania stirred his second cup of coffee. "Because you're new in America, between the two of us, if I were you, I would be looking for a safer job." He held his nostrils with his fingers, as if sighting a skunk. "He stinks; his father is worse."

"What do you know? I just left Sicily to get away from that sort of thing, and here I am."

"Don't worry, Ray. My father told me about you Grecos. You're good people. I'm glad to have met you. Call on me for anything you need."

What unsettled Ray most wasn't physical strength, but character, especially that of weak-minded people. Although Concetta held a tough job dealing with the public, to him she seemed vulnerable, a walking tragedy. Ray never visited the Catania family again. He always felt for her weakness. He wished he could have helped.

As for his own job, Ray was a recruiter for dressmakers. He worked a five-day week from morning to noon, a schedule that fit well with the new enterprise's activities. His boss, as Mr. Catania pointed out, was none other than a declining mobster's son who spent most of his days defending his business' legitimacy.

In his position, Ray provided jobs for lots of people in Bushwick, giving him plenty of clout, especially among those who didn't speak English. He became respectable indeed and the most sought-after person in the neighborhood. Because he played straight, the locals trusted him; it was the kind of trust he needed for his underground work.

By the end of his second year in the States, Ray had gone to work for another company. It was the largest fashion house of the day. The company was legitimate and fell within Don Saverio's rule, no Mafia links. He would work for this company for five years, spending the last two as a production manager. Here he would gain excellent experience.

With Silvana moving to Manhattan soon to head Giglio and the Class of '56 out of college, from behind the scenes, Ray would start expanding Giglio to the fullest, starting the race to the top.

11

NINETEEN SIXTY-THREE WAS A YEAR OF REVELATION for Mafia and politics as well. The general mood among Mafia members was somewhat somber for those who had been accused, and defiant for those still seeking recognition.

In the front room of Club Calatafimi in the early afternoon, over a cup of coffee, two senior members were debating the latest events from the comfort of their armchairs. Gino looked past Dominick's shoulder at a stranger mingling with members. "Dominick, did you watch Joe Vallaci on television last night?"

"You mean the squealer? Can you imagine that? He revealed *cosa nostra* on primetime for the world to hear."

"He's got some nerve. Before these hearings are over, he's going to get a bullet between his eyes."

"I agree. After what he did to *cosa nostra*—if I were younger, I'd shoot him myself."

"It's too late, Dominick. I can see him spilling the beans. After all, the boys didn't do much right by him either. After thirty years, they dropped him like a hot potato. But *cosa nostra*?"

Gino bit his lower lip, and his face paled. "He should've never touched that. That's like talking about your mother's sex life in public. That's not right."

Dominick gulped down a mouthful of coffee. "Look, Joe was in a bad fix with no way out. He had no choice but to turn informant."

Gino forced a smile. "Wait! Hold your thoughts for a second. I heard John DeMaria's name mentioned a few times the other day and never again. Do you know this guy?"

"No, can't say I do. Anyhow, Gino, how do you think those Mafia bosses feel about Joe spilling his guts?"

"I tell you, every time Joe opens his mouth, I bet they wet their pants. They never know what's next."

"That's nothing. I bet they squirmed when the committee showed all those organizational charts. And those guys on the committee can play the game better than any Mafia boss I've seen. They act as if they were trained in Sicily somewhere."

"I think those bosses deserve what's coming to them. I just don't think Joe Vallaci should walk away scot-free into the FBI program and start all over. He should get a dose of his own medicine. Once the committee's done, they should send him down the tube with the rest of them. That's what I think is going to happen anyhow."

"To hell with them all," intervened the stranger who had been listening. "This is America. They've put all Italians through some hell of shame."

"What's your name?"

"Vito Catania. I'm not a member yet. Sorry for the outburst; I just can't stand that kind of trash."

Dominick stared at him for a short moment. "Mr. Catania, you seem to know your stuff. Tell me, what do you think is going on with Bobby Kennedy and Jimmy Hoffa?"

"For my money, I think Kennedy's zeal got his brother killed. Again, that's my opinion."

Gino nodded. "I think so, too. You know what's funny. The head of the FBI . . . " He snapped his fingers for help. "What's his name?"

"J. Edgar Hoover."

"Oh yes. Hoover. Thanks, Dominick. That son of a bitch, he finally admitted that organized crime exists in America."

Mr. Catania swept a glance across the room. "That's a laugh."

Gino couldn't resist showing off his knowledge. "I know, and guess what? He's going to launch a war against organized crime. I thought only the president could declare war."

Dominick also felt the need to show off. "You know what's amazing? In the end, neither Fidel Castro nor the Kennedys will have any use for mobsters. With big business' help, politicians are organizing themselves better than Mafia."

Gino swung his armchair upright. "And who's going to touch these politicians now, God? I don't think so. Like you said, they're the ones who are legalizing Mafia."

In most Italian clubs, the controversial and speculative discussions about the hearings continued. For the first time, *cosa nostra* had been revealed to the public. The hearings drove most debaters to a euphoric state, showing a genuine sense of pride in their fight against organized crime. They were ready to condemn any informant to death. As for Don Saverio, who followed the demise of old Mafia from abroad, he simply smiled.

The poker game was well underway. From the front room, one could hear the prelude to the next round.

"I take two."

"I take one."

"I'm out."

"Dealer takes none."

A Tiffany fixture hanging from the ceiling dimly lit the players' faces: yellowish-green, with deep wrinkles around their mouths. They were engulfed in cigarette smoke. They wore their weariness with pride. The first round of bets raised the pot to five hundred dollars. The sum was too much to bear for the mostly jobless level-three players.

Most social clubs in the area had four levels of play. The first level consisted of members seeking to meet local politicians. In the front room, during daylight hours and early evening, they would engage in a casual game or two of penny-ante rummy, pinochle, or, for the old-timers, *briscola*.

The second level usually played from six to ten at night and were the working members. They'd stretch it to eleven o'clock if they were on a winning streak, or if they thought a chance at getting even might be coming their way. Besides gambling, their interest was in the number of nights out the club offered. This group played rummy for a couple of dollars and seven-card poker with a twenty-five-cent ante. Anything above that went to level three, the 10 p.m. to 1 a.m. crowd whose aspiration was to one day play with the high rollers and fix all their problems at once.

Of the last two levels, most players could not afford to lose more than a round without affecting their families' welfare. Yet most of them went on gambling, either to try to win enough to feed their families or to win back their losses. Around 2 a.m., the high rollers would stroll in as most of the level-three gamblers, dissolute and empty-handed, filed out for home. Others, whose respect was also a prize for the high rollers to win, stayed behind as spectators.

Thanks to Nino Maltese, Ray Greco became a spectator in social clubs. The twenty-nine-year-old Nino was not a gambler per se. He was the son of a couple Ray had provided a steady job to with fringe benefits and a good shot at a pension, too. Nino, a devoted son and an avid club-goer, kept himself very much up-to-date on Mafia gossip. He went to social clubs more often than he visited his church.

Nino led Ray out of the smoke-filled room.

"Tonight is going to be some hell of a night here."

"Why, Nino?"

"Let's sit down first."

"Before we sit, let me ask what's wrong with these clubs?"

"What do you mean?"

"They make you feel like a Martian."

Each sat on a recliner by the picture window that faced the street.

"Ray, that's a cultural thing, especially with Sicilians in America. Unless you come from the same community, you might as well be from a different planet. Get used to it."

"Uh-huh!"

Nino looked out at the approaching darkness. "Brooklyn is a large city with people from all over the world. You'll get used to . . . you'll see. Besides, not everyone can be from your town."

"Nino, you really know your way around; if it wasn't for you, I don't think I would've set foot in any club."

The bald club keeper approached Nino. "Hi, Mr. Nino, what can I get you?"

"Don Mario, is it too early for a rum and coke?"

"If you don't tell, I won't tell."

"Okay then. Two cokes on the rocks with a twist of lemon."

"Isn't liquor a good business for these guys?"

"It sure is, Ray! These club keepers can't live on tips alone. You know how it is, don't you?"

"No. I don't. What's his real job?"

"Don Mario collects the house cuts and keeps the games going with fresh cards and refreshments. If the take is good, he serves free pizza. What do you expect from a seventy-year-old man?"

As Nino continued rambling about club keepers, Ray was debating with himself whether or not to leave. He decided to stay a while longer.

"Remember, Don Mario, like most other club keepers at one time, were trusted people for their tight lips. But thanks to Joe Vallaci, they lost a lot of income in the way of tips from the big guys. Mafia meetings in clubs are things of the past. And maybe because of Joe, more club keepers are loosening their lips now."

"What's there to say? That's the old Mafia syndrome."

Nino rose halfway up his recliner.

"What're you talking about? . . . I tell you, you definitely know something I don't. Something is fishy, and I don't know what."

"Stop the nonsense, would you? This Don Mario, where is he from . . . and where are the drinks?"

Nino stared back at Ray. "He . . . he's from Calatafimi."

For the first time, Ray began to doubt his ability to find Santo, much less find the true story. He also wondered if he was being sucked into a world he didn't want to be in. He didn't complain, though; he had decided to see it through.

Seven years had passed since his arrival in the United States, and time was running out. As the new enterprise was taking hold, he didn't have much time to spend in Bushwick. To carry out Don Saverio's agenda, he spent most afternoons in Manhattan meeting heads of Mafia and other respectable people. Besides, there was his mother to settle by his side, his marriage to Silvana, and the expansion of Giglio Enterprises to come. Not to mention the Class of '56 was graduating from college soon.

Grandpa was right. Santo is slick; he moves around leaving no traces. But no man is an island. I'll get that son of a bitch if it's the last thing I do. Patience and perseverance were Ray's best allies. For the sake of finding Santo, he even put up with Nino's Mafia stories as they club-hopped on late nights.

Don Mario finally placed two cokes with rum and lemon peel on the coffee table and hurried to the back room.

Ray twisted the peel in his drink. "Nino, what's so special about tonight?"

"I don't know if I can trust you with this one."

"Why not?"

"Something's wrong. You being born in Sicily and all, at times it sounds like you're afraid of Mafia. Other times as if you were a Mafia boss. I just don't get it. Either you're pulling my leg or you're full of hot air. Something has to give. Deep inside I got these funny vibes, you know what I mean?"

Ray discounted Nino's assertion with a single wave of his hand. "You've got the whole thing wrong. It's not that I don't like Mafia stories. Lately my mind is on my job, the remodeling of the house, and on getting married, you know life-altering stuff. It's not easy. Trust me, it's not."

Puzzled, Nino looked at him.

Ray cleared his throat. "Nino, I would admit though, like most people, I like to peek into the world of Mafia. By the way, being a Sicilian doesn't automatically make me a Mafia man, although at times I wish I were. But I'm very much impressed with your Mafia connections. Someday I might come to you for help."

"We'll see. Tonight, they're expecting Mickey the Cat."

Before Ray asked, "Who the hell is Mickey the Cat?" Nino filled in the blanks. "Mickey Argento, to be exact, he's the most feared and highly paid hit man. Rumor has it that until Marcello had that nut

Oswald hit Kennedy, Mickey held that contract. Some say that Mickey is now holding an open-ended contract on Joe Vallaci."

"I never heard of Argento or Mickey the Cat. . . . Where's he from?"

"He's from Calatafimi. I understand he was nicknamed Argento for his shiny silvery hair when he first arrived in America."

"And where does the name Mickey the Cat come from?"

Nino laughed. "I guess a second nickname he earned for his trade; sort of a cat chasing a mouse. Why don't we ask him when he shows up?"

"What does he look like?"

Nino ordered another drink and a coffee for Ray. Then he talked like a fashion magazine gossip. "He has a tall, slim body. A full head of hair, like yours, polished silvery with no streaks."

Ray thought, *I know I'll be rewarded somehow for this torture.*

"Two-thirds of his hair is perfectly styled over his forehead like a visor, the rest neatly parted to his right. I tell you, Ray, this guy can model with the best. Anyone who knows him says the same thing. You've got to watch out for Mickey. His whole demeanor, with his blue eyes and soft smile, draws you into a certain kind of intimacy that makes you tell him all he wants to know and more. In that moment, if you look deep in his eyes, you see a man bragging about how many men he killed, same as a hunter brags about how many deer he's hunted down. That's his trade, killing people for money."

Ray took another sip of coffee and smiled.

"I tell you, Ray, he can lure anyone who lays an eye on him. I kid you not. He's a powerful figure."

Ray stopped quizzing Nino who, getting drunker, was beginning to act brave and silly at the same time. *Nino's compulsive need to gossip about Mafia intrigues*, thought Ray, *can only be attributed to some form of freedom he is trying to obtain.* Nevertheless, regardless of what kind of freedom, Nino was dangerous to Ray's future. Despite the back room's clamor, Ray closed his eyes and stretched back on the recliner, thinking about Mickey.

Ray awoke at ten minutes to one. He rushed to the men's room, refreshed himself, and then returned to the recliner and pretended to sleep. Nino was snoozing away the rum. At one o'clock, Mickey entered the club in a sandy-colored suit with a light blue long-sleeved shirt, silver cufflinks, and a burgundy tie. He scanned the room, paused for a second to glance at the two men sleeping on the recliners, and walked toward the back room. Peeking through his eyelashes, Ray recognized Mickey just as Nino had described him.

Stopping at the club keeper's post, Mickey bent down to collect a friendly hug and a thick envelope from Don Mario. His arrogant eyes roamed the crowd. He then walked toward a table where three players were setting up the game. The spectators began to circle the table.

No man of good judgment would imagine that under that well-presented body laid a cold assassin for hire. His speech was calm and deliberate, and he left no illusion as to the meaning of each word he spoke. In the nature of his business, everything he did was preplanned. He traveled alone and had only a few close friends. These were his only link to the world of Mafia, and because they brought him business, he kept in touch with them regularly. Other than that, Mickey retreated into his own world as an average family man where no one would believe he could hurt a fly.

Ray was impressed with the degree of accuracy with which Nino described Mickey, but he was not impressed with Mickey the man. In that business, hit men are traded as commodities, and they are not worthy of respect.

As Nino woke up, Don Mario brought six new decks of cards to the table. The butcher sat across from Mickey and the bookie across from the tailor. The bookie randomly picked up a deck and handed it to the butcher, who ripped the cellophane and took out all the twos, threes, fours, and jokers. Aces were played high and low.

With spectators at a safe distance, and four five-hundred-dollar antes in the pot, Mickey was about to deal the first round. But he went over the rules:

"A pair of jacks or better opens. The most you can open with is a thousand dollars. You can raise twice on the first go-around. After discard, you can open with two thousand and raise three times. Check and raise, it's okay."

The tailor cut the deck, and Mickey dealt the first hand. For the first two hours, the game went by without incident, with the house winning. Ray looked at Nino, disappointed. Hoping to deliver on his promise, Nino insisted things would warm up. They were dealing the last hand. Ray and Nino stood behind Mickey. After Nino's tales about Mickey, Ray decided not to look into his eyes.

The tailor, the first to bet, checked.

Mickey opened with a thousand dollars.

The bookie saw the thousand, and the butcher raised the ante to two thousand.

The tailor pushed his two thousand in, and Mickey raised another thousand.

With all bets in at an even three thousand dollars each, the tailor declared himself served and took no cards.

Mickey took one card, the bookie one, and the butcher three.

"Opener talks," said the butcher.

"Opener bets two thousand," said Mickey without hesitation.

"I . . . I'm in," said the bookie.

"He might as well fold," Nino whispered.

Ray shrugged his shoulders.

The butcher rechecked his hand.

"I'll see your two thousand and raise another two."

The tailor studied the table for a moment, and then pushed his four thousand in.

At this point, no matter how closely the spectators watched, no one had an angle on any player's hand. Gamblers rarely had to glance at more than a bitty part of their cards. Some of these players spent a lifetime learning how to read cards in such a way that others couldn't even see the color of the suit.

Mickey looked at the butcher. "I'll see your two thousand and raise you another two."

The bookie, with a straight going in, folded.

The butcher rebuffed Mickey's bet by raising another two thousand.

Disgusted, the tailor, with a flush served, folded.

Mickey matched the butcher's two thousand dollar raise. Then looked at the butcher. "Now that we're alone, why not spice up the ante by another ten thousand?"

The butcher paused for a brief second. "Sure, why not? Let's see what you got."

The pot was a whopping fifty-six thousand dollars, including the antes. Mickey laid one king after another on the table and said, "I culled a card just for show. These four gentlemen made my hand right from the start."

"If you don't want your hand chopped off here and now, I suggest you leave it right there," said the butcher as Mickey reached out for the pot and he for his six-inch blade.

In that suspended moment, Ray noticed Mickey's left hand and realized that, after all these years, he was finally standing only two feet behind Santo Pellegrino. He wanted to act right then and there, but he had trained long and hard not to spoil moments like these.

To Mickey's surprise and all the spectators', the butcher had assembled four aces.

Santo Pellegrino, alias Mickey the Cat, was slick, was not from Alcamo, was missing his left forefinger, and, above all, was a gambler.

On the night before Christmas, Ray walked home with different priorities.

12

IN GOOD COMPANY, NEW YEAR'S EVE IN MANHATTAN can be the most exciting night of the year. Ray had reserved a table at Tavern on the Green. Dressed like Eskimos ready to attack a blizzard, they left Silvana's Thirty-third Street apartment at seven-thirty. Tonight, walking to Central Park seemed to be Silvana's secret pilgrimage.

She held on to Ray's arm. "Ray, there's nothing better than a brisk walk to the park."

He watched the two steam jets drifting from her nostrils. "I don't know what's so good."

"I feel invigorated, fresh air going through my lungs . . . blood rushing . . . "

"Save it, Silvana! The only thing I feel is your body shivering and my nose about to freeze, and there are two dozen more blocks to go. If we ever make it alive, the party will be over, and at best, they'll have to thaw us back to life. Forget it. This is nuts! I'm getting a cab."

She chattered her teeth to the tune of "Jingle Bells." "I'm looking, Ray."

An hour after they started walking, they hailed the only cab in sight, with no luck. The next fifteen minutes were the most miserable. Finally, a shiny yellow limousine beeped the horn and pulled over. It wasn't until they got in the backseat that they realized it was a rattling old cab, a lifesaver nevertheless. Through the rear window, Ray saw a blanket of scattered clouds. When he leaned back, he saw never-ending rows of lights reflecting off the tall buildings that surrounded the park. The roundabout motion of the cab against the swirling view reminded Ray of the carnival rides he used to take as a little boy with his father. This time, though, he got dizzy and the ride was with Silvana on the largest merry-go-round in the world, Central Park.

They arrived with a half-hour to spare; the hostess led them to their table. Before they could settle into their chairs, a well-tailored elderly waiter with a wan smile announced, "My name is Dick; may I take your drink orders?"

When Ray screwed up his face, Silvana knew the waiter was in trouble. Ray disliked it when people messed with their own names—or in this case, did nothing to improve on them. "Dick" and "drinks" in the same sentence did not sit well with Ray, but he was in a joyful mood.

With a reputation for not knowing the difference between scotch and milk, Ray showed off what he had learned a few nights earlier. He ordered two cokes on the rocks with rum and a twist of lemon. She was impressed. The grinning waiter was not and had the same demeanor when he got back with the drinks.

Silvana twirled her drink with a straw. "When are you giving up the apartment in Brooklyn, Ray?"

"Give it up? I just bought the whole house. I'm kicking the two tenants out, and I start remodeling in a few weeks. I'll double the rent. It's a good investment, you'll see."

"What about us?"

"What about us!"

"Aren't we getting married in April?"

"That's right, April 10."

"And we're moving into my apartment, right?"

"That's right! What's bothering you?"

"Ray! I don't want to live in Brooklyn."

"Neither do I."

He shifted his drink from one hand to the other.

"Don't get all riled up for nothing. Okay?"

She just looked at him.

"The buying of the house has nothing to do with our wedding plans. I only bought it for business and sentimental reasons."

"What sentimental reasons? Is there something I should know?"

"Sherlock, there's nothing you don't know already. I spent seven years in that apartment. Besides, it'll help me stay in touch with friends."

"I'm not Sherlock Holmes, but I understand now. When did you decide to buy the house?"

"The night before Christmas."

Dick went back to his station twice empty-handed before the others arrived. When Victor and his girlfriend showed up, Ray stood up, as Silvana looked at her low-cut double-breasted red outfit.

"Hi, Victor. I'm glad you made it too, Nora.

"Silvana, this is Nora, Victor's girlfriend. Please sit down."

As the excitement at the restaurant began to build, Marco and Angelo joined the table. Unbeknownst to Nora, Marco had hinted that Silvana take her away from the table for a while. Smiling at his plea, she asked Nora to accompany her to the powder room. With the girls only a few steps away, Marco asked, "Why the tail, Victor?"

"What's the difference? We couldn't have talked with Silvana present anyhow. Besides, she was invited, and I didn't know of any hot topics tonight."

Ray intervened. "Victor's right. I invited her. Now, before they come back, let me tell you, Victor, your ex-girlfriend, Gina, is making trouble for Carlo."

"How's that Ray?"

"What did she have to do with Carlo?" asked Marco.

"Where's she now?" Victor wanted to know.

"One at a time, guys. The only thing I know is that Benito Campo, Gloria's brother, all grown up now, is asking lots of questions."

"What's Carlo saying?"

"I haven't heard from him yet, Victor."

"I sense trouble," said Angelo.

"May I bring another round of—"

Ray glared the waiter. "Listen, Dick, if you show your stupid face here once . . . better yet, have someone else serve this table."

As Dick left, they all burst out laughing.

"Why did you call him 'dick?'" asked Victor, somewhat composed now.

"That's his name. Don't you get it? I bet his real name is Richard."

Ray got back to business. "Angelo, how's your deal with the insurance company coming along?"

"The people at Hartford wouldn't take 'no' for an answer. They're in love with my credentials. So I took a job as a junior construction loan specialist. After a year of training, I'll head my own department and then, hopefully, the company."

"What about you, Marco? How are you doing on the Hill?"

"Well, I'll tell you, with Lyndon Johnson and Lady Bird in the White House, the word is that Bobby Kennedy and company are out. LBJ hates his guts. With Bobby out and the administration in turmoil, we'll position our people in the right places. For myself, I have a job in the House of Representatives where I can do the most good."

"I hope so. You sound like a politician already. From now on, we have a bunch of new guys coming out of college every year looking for places to go. How about you, Victor?"

"I'm doing fine. The Coast is a place on the go. I'm working on two hot deals. Soon I'll know enough to decide. In the meantime, I'm doing consulting work for some start-up companies. I'll let you know as soon as I decide which deal is best. We'll work things out. I don't think either deal will take much to close."

Ray felt obliged to report on the state of the Class of '56.

"I didn't want to take a chance with us all meeting in one place. The others are doing fine. Luca and Paul are setting themselves up nicely in the credit card business. That industry is a much bigger deal than anyone thought . . . and growing. I think Don Saverio hit the nail right on the head with that one. By the way, keep an eye open for anything on this credit card deal. You never know what else is lurking out there.

"For myself, let me say, next month I'll start full time at Giglio. So far, I've secured shelf space for the new season in over eight thousand fashion outlets. Through a line of subcontractors, we anticipate going into full production by the middle of next year. Since Silvana arrived in New York, she and her staff have worked at new creations and gradually increased sales, which is essential for a good business foundation. But the time has come to get it up to speed."

Ray watched Silvana make her way back to the table with Nora. "Look at her; everyone is looking at her outfit in awe. I tell you . . . she's good. Can you believe she made that entire outfit at the last moment and almost out of nothing?"

Ray got back on track with a sense of contentment. "Soon I'll hire more office help just for back-room operations. Silvana and I will handle marketing with some serious publicists and advertising agents from here in Manhattan. We've already secured copyrights and company trademarks. As we move along, I'm sure I'll need your help. Now, let's stop talking business and celebrate the new year."

Silvana and Nora checked in just in time to pose for the house photographer, a voluptuous girl who had enticed Ray and the others into taking a few photos. A young waiter politely asked Silvana if she cared for a fresh drink.

"No thanks. But refill the others, please."

When she asked "what happened to Dick," she needed no account, for they all broke down laughing again.

At the center of the table, a silver tray cradled a golden turkey. It was surrounded with platters and bowls filled with dressing, potatoes, gravy, cranberry sauce, vegetables, fruits, and hot rolls. Three buckets of ice held bottles of wine and champagne. Ray sat at one end of the table and Silvana at the other. He surveyed the spread for a moment then tapped his glass with a knife to signal his approval.

For Ray, the homey feeling didn't come from the taste of the food but in the after-meal pleasure of being with his own. The rushed clearing of the table saddened Ray deeply, for it signaled the end of good times. When people gathered, a cluttered table was much cozier than an orderly or empty one. After this sort of dinner, free of table manners, it was a pleasure to reach for another piece of cheese, a stalk of celery, or some other leftover; especially that last cup of coffee accompanied by good conversation.

With the giggles of women accenting the festivities, the evening galloped toward midnight. With glass in hand and Santo in mind, Ray proposed a toast to better things to come.

The talk now focused on the wedding. In keeping with her father's plan, Silvana had moved to Manhattan and adopted Ray's last name. In the world of fashion, people already knew her as Silvana Greco.

"Did you set a wedding date yet?"

"Yes, Nora, April 10, here at City Hall."

"Why at City Hall?"

Ray pierced an olive with a toothpick. "Convenience and legality. The marriage license will take the INS off her back, and the low-key ceremony will hopefully keep things quiet."

"What about the church?"

"There is none. It's all at City Hall."

With most wedding questions out of the way and a clear mission established, Silvana walked around the table and waved her finger under Ray's nose. "When you hear our tune, you and I are dancing."

"Yes, ma'am!"

"You had it coming," laughed Victor, as he headed for the dance floor with Nora.

Next the band played "Love Is a Many-Splendored Thing." Jubilant, Silvana rushed Ray to the floor and danced.

A few hours into 1964, with the New Year's Eve party behind them and new resolve for the future, Ray walked Silvana all the way back to her apartment for a celebration of their own. This time, although the temperature had dropped several degrees since their earlier attempt, they felt no cold.

13

THAT INFAMOUS AUGUST 31 changed the exciting life of eighteen-year-old Gina into one of seclusion, despair, and fear. Since the incident, she had refused to speak about her ordeal with anyone. Today, seven years after the slaughter of Gloria and Stefano, she agreed to tell all to Benito Campo, Gloria's brother.

The sheer curtains in the living room window dimmed the afternoon sunlight. Benito sat at the left end of the sofa waiting anxiously. Fragile and pale, Gina walked into the small living room, sat at the other end of the sofa, and pulled her skirt tight over her knees.

"Hi, Gina."

"Benito, I never thought I would do this. It isn't going to be easy . . . Please, bear with me."

He smiled.

"That night I was watching from behind the stone wall across the bungalow. Two men were holding Stefano, and two others had Gloria. Stefano shouted, 'Carlo, what're you doing? Who are these guys? Leave her alone. You know she's carrying your baby, for God's sake, stop!'

"He was no match for them. They knocked her out with a single blow to the head and stripped her naked."

Benito got the first bitter taste of truth. His eyelids quivered. "Don't mind me, blood is blood. I was only fifteen. I loved my sister. I need to know and feel everything she felt. Please go on."

"I don't know how you can take it."

"Gina, I'm not afraid of the truth."

Blinded by tears, she stared at the far wall. "My date with Victor wasn't for another hour. I was infatuated and counted every minute of the day waiting for the date. When I grew impatient, I went to the bottom of the hill to wait for him there. If I'd only waited a little longer, I would've missed the whole thing."

Benito laid his handkerchief next to her.

"Thanks, I'll be okay." She dabbed her eyes.

Gina was standing by the shack's railing and night had fallen, when she heard faint voices coming from a little way up the hill. She moved within earshot. When Stefano pushed the window of the shack open to let some breeze in, what Gina saw was an unframed single bed, a desk, a bookcase, an armoire, and a wicker chair that Gloria was sitting on. The walls were bare.

Stefano, twenty-six, Don Saverio's older son, had a strong-boned face with a head of black hair parted near the middle, revealing the intellectual man that he was. Behind his easy-going attitude, he concealed a brilliant mind. Like his sister, he was anti-tradition, and he didn't approve of his family's business. All summer he had acted as a friend and a mentor to Gloria, who had fallen out of love with his brother, Carlo.

Stefano was leaning against the window facing Gloria. She got up, "Stefano, I don't know how to thank you for listening to me."

"That's okay; I'm glad I can help."

"Carlo said get an abortion or else . . ."

"Don't even think of it. We'll find a solution."

"That's well and good. But in this town, with a baby and no husband . . . " She pulled out a letter from her skirt pocket. "My cousin from Roma wrote me yesterday. She moved there with her husband two years ago to look for a better job. She's very excited about my going there. She even found me a temporary job."

"Well, that's a start."

"She talked it over with her husband. I know it will be a heartbreaker for my brother, but he can join me after the baby is born. For now, the baby comes first. Benito will understand. Why do I tell you all this? Please don't tell Carlo. I just want him to leave me alone."

"Don't worry; you go ahead. If I have to, I'll speak with my father. He's a reasonable man."

"I don't think so. Your father, like your brother, is more concerned about family honor than my problem."

"You might be right . . ."

"I know I'm right. Your brother is not the guy he used to be. I don't understand him anymore."

"My brother and I used to share secrets and help each other out. Now, every time I talk to him, he looks at me cockeyed and walks away. My father is acting the same way. Frankly, I don't know what to make of it."

"The other night I had this off-and-on-dream of Carlo telling your father about us having an affair. Then, laughing like a wild joker, Carlo made you disappear so he could become the next in line to inherit the kingdom. Your father was dressed like a king with a crown on his head that read: "Don Saverio, King of Mafia." The terrifying part was when Carlo managed to push me, your father, and his grandchild into an inferno-like crevasse spewing flames."

"Everything makes sense now; please Gloria, say no more. Let's get out of here. Knowing Carlo, tonight is the perfect time. These people are capable of anything. They'll turn on their own mothers, no less a brother or a son."

She was terrified.

Stefano pushed himself off the window frame.

"Gloria, I'm afraid your dream is an omen. Everything is coming together now. How can he ever think that we are cheating on him? How can he?"

"He can!"

He looked out the window, distressed. "I've got to clear things up with my father before it's too late. Let's get out of here. I think that you, the baby, and I are in his way. Let's go. Everything makes sense now."

Stefano grabbed her arm and headed for the door but stopped short.

Gina pulled back behind the stone wall, terrified. There were two men, shotguns in hand, crouched under the window and two others by the door. In a flash, there was Carlo.

Benito nodded impatiently.

Gina stared at the wall still, unaware of Benito's blushing rage. "Benito, I have to tell you, I was truly terrified."

Carlo and two men burst into the room as the others jumped in through the window and got hold of Stefano. Very much aware of his predicament, Stefano desperately tried to calm his brother down. A single blow knocked Gloria out. Then Carlo shouted, "You son of a bitch. You've been screwing her all summer long and now you want me to stop? By the time this is over," pointing the shotgun toward her limp body, "there will be nothing left for you to screw or take over. Trust me, idiot!"

"Take over what . . .? Does Dad know you're here?"

"Who the hell do you think sent me?"

"You bastard!" he cried out as he wrestled to free himself. "You planned the whole thing, you bastard! Why do all this? You know how I feel about our family business! You're a degenerate, you're insane—"

Before Stefano could finish his sentence, the man behind him plunged the butt of his shotgun into Stefano's neck with such force that his head started bobbing as if dangling from a rubber band.

They stripped him from the waist down and sat him on the wicker chair with his head thrown back. Carlo nonchalantly thanked the men and said, "You guys better go; Calatafimi is a long way out. I'll take care of the rest." As Carlo waved the men good-bye, the breeze carried the tune of "Jezebel" from the villa. He walked back inside and looked at Gloria. He spread her legs a little with the tip of the shotgun. He knelt on one knee at the foot of the bed. He shoved the double barrel in her vagina. "Didn't I tell you to get an abortion?"

He pulled the trigger. Her body jolted once, but did not splatter. With shotgun in hand, he walked toward his brother, placed the double barrel in his mouth, and pulled the trigger again. The song stopped playing. Carlo surveyed the scene, placed the shotgun in Stefano's hands, wiped his own hands clean, then calmly walked back to the villa.

Gina glanced at Benito. He blinked a few times, gritted his teeth, nodded, shook his head, and looked away.

Tears rolled down her cheeks. "Now, the only thing I see in my dreams is Gloria and Stefano walking out of the front door begging for help. Back then, I thought of Victor, so I ran to him. At first I tried to explain but then . . . I can't recall."

It was that sudden, insatiable carnal desire that drove her to a mad lovemaking session. That was Gina's first and last sexual experience, and she had no recollection of it.

The sun was setting when Benito shut the door behind him, and Gina's anxieties were much relieved for having shared her ordeal with someone.

On a Sunday afternoon, Piazza Ciullo is what every town square should be: crowded and peaceful at the same time, men meeting at sidewalk cafés. Here, over a cup of coffee or two, they talk about life's struggle. Most women in Alcamo rarely participated in this event, for they understood their men, or so they thought. They usually joined them in the early evenings for a stroll down the *corso* or to go and visit relatives. In short, Alcamo's Sunday afternoons are men's time-outs.

The larger of the two cafés in the *piazza* had eight four-chair tables. The café, with a patio-like setting, was in full view of the crowd. Carlo Cremona and two of his men sat at one table, facing the square.

Benito's investment in informers had panned out. He was disappointed, though, since only two of the four men showed up. Resigned, he entered the café from the side door and came out the front walking behind a waiter. When he reached Carlo's table, before they could run for cover, Benito shot the man to Carlo's right and then the other in the blink of an eye. Then, before the terrified looks of the customers, with the other men slumped dead in their chairs, he pointed the gun at Carlo's head.

Carlo cried out, "Benito, no! It . . . it wasn't me; I loved Gloria. Your sister was—"

"You lying bastard!" said Benito as he pulled the trigger. Then he walked calmly around the table, knocked Carlo to the floor, and kicked him over, checking for any signs of life. He stared at the crowd, raised the gun to his temple, and pulled the trigger a final time.

As a man of honor, Benito Campo knew he was doomed to die. And for that, people revere him still.

14

THE CHAPEL FOR THE TWO O'CLOCK CEREMONY at City Hall was ready. The justice of the peace was Jewish, and the best man was Irish. When the clerk called in the Greco party, the only guests present were Sergio and his wife and Pat O'Brien and his girlfriend. Sergio was Giglio's controller and Pat the marketing man.

A traffic jam on the Williamsburg Bridge delayed two limousines. The first carried Silvana, Ray, his mother, and her new husband, Sal. The other carried Victor, Nora, Angelo, and Marco. The thing Ray hated most—being late—was happening to him at his own wedding. Don Saverio and his family, owing to Carlo's death, had excused themselves from attending. But Ray knew better. To pursue his own agenda, since Carlo's death, Ray had taken over Mafia's good and bad activities in America.

The two limousines were at a standstill in the westbound lane. Looking out over the city, Sal wondered who had created the chaos of skyscrapers, streets, elevated roads, and bridges. In that intimidating atmosphere, Sal thought, *They must have done it while God was sleeping.* What concerned him more, though, was the heavy smog; he could barely see the Brooklyn Bridge, much less the Fifty-ninth Street Bridge just further north, spanning the East River.

Somewhat jealous of Sal, Ray sat in the tight quarters facing his mother and Sal. Although he favored their marriage and respected Sal as family, he wondered why his mother had traded a life in New York City near him for one in Alcamo with Sal. Who am I to understand women? Even my mother, he thought.

Envisioning the man who once sat on a mound cracking stones, Ray could not accept Sal as his mother's lover. No matter how much he liked Sal, he found any of his gestures of intimacy toward his mother repulsive. However, as with all other emotions, Ray thought he would learn how to deal with that one, too.

The fifty-year-old Sal Rocca, a burly man of medium height, was not, nor had he ever been, a handsome man. On the contrary, he had a square, sun-hardened face with kind eyes and a flattened nose that seemed to hold no bone. His thick black hair, ready to spring up in all directions when dry, was held in place with a greasy substance. His bushy mustache went lopsided when he smiled. In spite of it all, because he was soft-spoken and had an easy, informal manner, he had sex appeal.

An ex-businessman, he took a job as a pieceworker with the Grecos in the aftermath of World War II. Sal was a man of honor. After Luciano's death, his loyalty to the Greco family and his good business sense placed him at the head of the firm owned by Ray and his mother.

A few years younger than Sal, Francesca was well educated and a very attractive woman. All things about her seemed strange to her son now. No longer tired, she pushed away the self-inflicted layers of suffering that had crept upon her following Luciano's death. Now, she revealed her deep beauty when she smiled. Ray was trying to recollect when he last saw her smile that way, but the stop and start of the traffic broke his thought.

Ray held Silvana's hand as he looked at Sal.

"Ray, we've been here only a day. With the exception of the spiral staircase in your apartment, so far I like everything. But just because I like it doesn't mean I'd live here. For a small-town person, it's too much. And I'm sure I'm speaking for your mother, too. If you think of us moving here, who would run the gravel business back home?"

The bridge was packed with cars and trucks. Silvana looked ahead. "If this traffic doesn't move soon, we'll have to walk off this bridge and get a cab."

Ray smiled. "Don't worry. Pat is a good talker. By now, I bet he made a deal with the judge to wait until midnight if he has to. Trust me."

With a backward glance, Ray noticed that the other limousine was only a bumper away. He turned to Sal. "How's the crusher working out?"

Before Sal could answer, Francesca intervened. "Sal is a genius. Right from the start, the crusher was a sight to behold. Trucks back up the ramp, dumping large stones into a chute. A pair of hydraulic jaws splits them into smaller pieces, allowing them to free-fall into another chamber where they are crushed into gravel. A conveyer collects and sorts it according to size into three different bins."

"Ma, you sound like an engineer. Since when have you even watched a hammer swing?"

She looked at Sal and smiled.

"Look, Ray. The day of hand labor is gone in Sicily. For my money, a mobile crusher is the way to go. We can set one up wherever gravel is used. What do you think?"

The traffic began to move.

"It makes sense, Sal. You'd better start working on it as soon as you get back to Alcamo, before someone else jumps on it. And while you're at it, start thinking about ready-mixed concrete. They're not going to mix concrete by hand much longer, either."

Under Ray's watchful eye, Sal smiled and squeezed Francesca's hand. Ray shook his head a bit and moved closer to Silvana. At the foot of the bridge, the limousines pulled straight ahead onto Delancey Street then turned left to City Hall.

It was three o'clock when they walked into the chapel. Twenty minutes later, Ray and Silvana were on their way back home as Mr. and Mrs. Ray Greco.

Two days after the wedding, Ray arranged for Sal to visit a ready-mixed concrete plant in Queens so he could be alone with his mother. It would take Sal the whole day, since he would check every nut and bolt in the plant.

Mother and son sat on the sofa, silently enjoying the moment.

"What do you think of this place?"

"Son, I like to stay on solid ground. The squeaking of wood as I walk through the apartment gives me the weird sensation of falling through the floor with every step I take."

He listened to every word she spoke in awe. To him, each word meant something different from its superficial meaning. He was satisfying seven years of hunger for motherly attention. And no matter what she said, or how she said it, he knew she meant no harm; they were words of wisdom that only he could understand and no other could deliver. So he willed her on.

"And that stupid stairway of yours . . . If you climb it too fast, it'll get you all bruised up. The other day, if it weren't for that card table by the window, I would've dropped a tray full of coffee cups and cookies. You'd better replace it with a wider marble staircase and take that one where it belongs, backstage in some old theater."

"Mom, the problem isn't the wooden floors or the spiral staircase. The problem is that marble is cheap in Sicily, depriving you of the warmth of carpeted floors and wooden walls. As for the spiral staircase, it came with the house. When I remodel the apartment, it will be the first thing to go. Anyhow, how's Grandpa?"

"Your grandfather is a great man. I'll always be indebted to him. He made me realize that my self-inflicted sorrow didn't only hurt me, but those who loved me as well. That's a lesson I'll never forget."

"How's Sal treating you?"

She patted his hand. "Calm down. I noticed how your face turned red when Sal held my hand. Although no one can ever fill your father's void, Sal is a caring, gentle man who fulfills me now. And, as I did, you must also let go of the past and pursue your dream."

He got up and walked to the window. "It's not that easy, Ma." He looked up past the rooftops. "I don't know what it is, but something is ingrained in me."

She looked at him, deep in thought.

"Ma, I'll try my best, I promise." He glanced back at her with a soft smile. "Besides, I love Sal. I've nothing but fond memories of him. Dad trusted him, and so do I. I guess it's the blood rebelling. I'll get used to it. I will."

Thinking of the man who put him in this predicament, relaxed and nervous at the same time, Ray sat next to his mother again. After a little while, he kissed her forehead and walked back to the window. She sensed his restlessness; she walked to his side and laid her head on his shoulder for a while, also looking out, then, squeezed his arm.

"Now that you asked about me . . . how are you doing? Or shall I ask, what are your plans as a married man?"

"After you leave, the first thing I'll do is spend my honeymoon with Silvana away from here. She wants to be here during your stay."

Francesca was edgy—she could never put out of her mind that Silvana was Don Saverio's daughter.

"She's a good girl, isn't she? . . . What about after the honeymoon?"

"She's been working hard at building up Giglio. She's agreed to slow down a bit to build a family. We want at least two children. We figured by the time she's needed back at work, the children should be in middle school. She can still design from home."

"What kind of a home are you talking about?"

"There's this place at the very tip of Long Island that reminds us of Alcamo Marina. Last month, visiting friends there, we found a nice house for sale. To make a long story short, she fell in love with it and we bought it."

She was about to question him when he corrected himself. "Don't say a word to Silvana. She wants to show it to you herself before you go back. She'll drive you there."

"How far is this place?"

"Quite a way, almost a three-hour ride."

"You'll spend your entire life on the road."

"No, I won't. I'll be going mostly on weekends. During the week, I'll stay here or at the office. I'll be okay, really. It's only for the summer, for Silvana and the kids."

"Does this house have a backyard?"

"Does it have a backyard? Wait until you see it! The house sits on a large fenced lot with an enclosed swimming pool and a veranda facing the ocean. It's the perfect summer place, you'll see. The kids will love it!"

Francesca, somewhat satisfied regarding the welfare of her future grandchildren, looked at her son and narrowed her eyes.

"What about Santo Pellegrino?"

"Who?"

"You heard me! Let bygones be bygones and get on with life. If you want to enjoy your family, you have to let it go. We are not that kind of people."

In that moment, the only thing he could see in his mind was the inscription on his father's grave: Luciano Greco lives through his son Ray and the promise he made: I'll get them. I promise I will.

On that bright spring morning, Silvana drove Francesca to Long Island. The apparent objective of the day was for Silvana to show Francesca the house and for Ray to visit Sal later that morning. The true objective, however, was for the two women to strengthen their relationship and for Ray and Sal to sign off on some ongoing business.

Driving through the streets of Brooklyn, Ray wondered how his mother knew about Santo. *She hasn't changed a bit, I guess. Like all mothers, they always know somehow. It wasn't Grandpa. He would never tell a woman.* Perhaps the mysterious thought fascinated Ray more than the truth of how she kept a step ahead of things.

Turning onto Harman Street, by force of habit he parked the car on what he thought was the lawful side of the street, but it was Saturday and no parking rules applied. Admiring the wax job the neighbor and his son had given to their '57 Chevy, he approached them, then smiling asked the kid. "How old are you?

"Nine."

"Do you know how to write?"

"Of course!" the kid said, with little quivers around his lips ready to break into a smile.

"Don't do as I did, give your father a rest, and don't forget those whitewall tires. Do a good job, and when I come down, I'll give you a buck."

"Wow!"

The father reached for the pail and the kid for the scrubbing brush. With the deal made, Ray went up the stoop and into the apartment. Smelling coffee, he went downstairs, making a rare appearance in the kitchen where Sal was brewing espresso with a percolator.

"Why didn't you ask? I would've brought my espresso machine. That's not coffee; that's tinted water."

"It'll satisfy the intent. If it weren't for that stupid staircase forcing you down here, you would've never seen me using the percolator. When it comes to taste, I know you well."

With coffees in hand, they made their way up the stairs to the card table. The see-through curtains subdued most of the daylight glare. They sat opposite each other. Ray, in his late twenties, was no longer the little boy who used to tap Sal's shoulder for a toy, but the head of Don Saverio's enterprises in America. Sal was the head of Greco Enterprises in Sicily.

Both men stared at each other in wonder, waiting for the other to speak first, but neither would. Ray confided in the only man he trusted. "The night before Christmas I spotted Santo."

"Did he see you?"

"He might have. Even if he did, it makes no difference."

"Your grandfather will be delighted to hear that. Since Santo left Sicily, no matter how we tried, we couldn't get a lead on him."

"How could you? Santo entered the United States with an illegal passport under the alias Mickey Argento, and was later nicknamed Mickey the Cat. I had Marco at the FBI check his passport. It was issued a month before my father was killed. We can surmise that Don Saverio set him up here. Back then, only a few heads of families knew about him. The more unknown the hit man is, the better."

"It all makes sense. Now it's time for you to step aside and let me handle this guy."

Ray looked out the window, shook his head slightly, searching for words. He spotted the sparkling whitewall tires and the kid playing stickball with his father. He saw himself as a little boy playing with his own father. Then he turned to Sal.

"No! It cannot be. This is my deal."

"Ray! You must be joking. There's too much at stake here; you never did this sort of thing."

"No. Never did, but I promised I will. There will be no other way. It's final."

"Okay, I won't argue with you. . . . When?"

"Not yet. Before I do anything, I've got to link Santo to the man who hired him."

"Good. But how?"

"Trust me, I know how. Before we make a move, I must do a few things."

"What do you want me to do?"

"For some strange reason, as recently as last December, I was hoping to find my father's murder justifiable. I wanted to believe that the man who ordered the killing was following some rule of *omertà*. Not so much so that I could quit, but to liberate the man who I think hired Santo, Don Saverio himself . . . perhaps a way of paying my dues for something . . . I don't really know."

"That's what your grandfather feared most when you were growing up in Alcamo. He never lost confidence in you, though. He always said, 'He's a Greco; leave him alone and he'll come through.'"

"Grandpa's right. When I first spotted Santo, standing only a couple of feet back from him, blood rushed to my head. At that moment, the only justifiable thing I could think of was to slaughter the son of a bitch right then and there with my bare hands."

Sal began to understand Ray's strategy.

"Acting on impulse is a mistake. I want to hear it all from Santo himself."

"And how are you going to do that?"

He looked out the window again, paused for a second. "We'll hire Santo to kill me."

"Get out of here! You're crazy!"

"No, I'm not!"

"We're dealing with a pro. It's too dangerous. Can't you think of another way?"

"No. There is no other way. I told you already. This is my deal. Now, if you listen, everything will work out just fine."

Sal stood by and clenched his teeth.

"If Don Saverio was the man who put the contract on my father, then Santo, believing he's getting another contract from him, will take this one, too. Only this time, it will be his last, as well as the beginning of the end for Don Saverio. When you go back next week, drive out to Calatafimi and see Don Nardo. Ask him for an introduction to Don Mario at the club for putting a contract on a guy from Brooklyn with someone that's not connected with us."

"What if he runs it past Don Saverio?"

"He won't. He knows I run the operations here. Besides, he thinks Santo is working out of the West Coast. Don Nardo will only be concerned with his cut. Put the money on the table first. He needs lots of cash these days, and he's too indebted to Don Saverio. Once he takes the money, although he should not, he'll never make mention of it to anyone, much less Don Saverio."

"Who do I say I am?"

"I'll make sure he'll be expecting you. By then, he won't care who you are as long as you give him the cash and say, 'Ray sent me.'

"You see, Don Mario will not call Santo unless Don Nardo approves the contract first.

"Don't worry. I can't afford my mother widowed again."

When Ray left the apartment, the kid sat at the bottom step looking up at him.

Ray reached in his pocket and gave the kid a dollar. "A deal is a deal. From now on, if you want to make more bucks, the only thing you've got to do is watch out for strangers looking at my place. If they drive a car, write down their license plate number and give it to me next time you see me. And above all, say nothing and don't take orders from anyone else."

"It's a deal!"

The kid ran across street.

15

LYNDON JOHNSON WAS PUSHING the Civil Rights Bill through Congress in 1964. He also declared war on poverty, and the Vietnam War was on the horizon. During that time, thanks to Bobby Kennedy leaving the post of attorney general, investigations into the mob dropped by 75 percent.

A month after his wedding, Ray laid out a plan for Giglio. Pat O'Brien was doodling on a pad of paper. Then he looked up. "Ray, I'm afraid your marketing plan might be too bold for the times."

Ray discounted Pat's statement briefly and looked at Sergio Bruno.

"Ray, don't look at me. I told you about Pat already. Frankly, I agree with him. America, and for that matter the world, is not ready for a fashion explosion. I say let's take a more prudent course at a slower pace. . . . What do you say?"

Pat turned his pad around. "Look, Ray, what concerns me most is we might lose it all . . . and for what? Maybe, if we get lucky, sales will increase. But that will hasten overgrowth, which leads to chaotic production. Again, for the life of me, I can't see the hurry."

Ray twirled the stub of a yellow pencil between his thumb and forefinger.

Pat went back to doodling.

Sergio stood silent, ready to debate the next speaker.

Two more twirls and Ray broke the silence. "I suggest that we start looking at Giglio as a fast-growing company. The sooner we get in that mind-set, the sooner we'll be able to handle the ups and downs."

Pat and Sergio looked at each other. They firmed up their lips, for they had no words.

"Face it, guys, no one's saying it's easy. But there comes a time when a decision has to be made. For Giglio, this is that time. I believe in this plan, and so does Silvana."

"Then . . . why not lay it all out for us?"

If there was a belief that Don Saverio had instilled in Ray, it was in creation and acceptance. And he did that while admiring nature with Ray on an autumn afternoon. "Watercolors, son, that's all it takes: a good base and a few colors."

Ray's plan had that and more. It had a good company, Silvana's successful creations, and the acceptance of at least one believer, himself.

"Guys, my contention is that there are no bad or good times for fashion, nor are there ugly or beautiful creations. There are only trends and styles with affordable price tags for the times. Fashion is created, not demanded. Since the masses will follow the few who set that trend, they will accept it most when it's associated with stylish people."

Ray's statement caused Pat and Sergio to readjust their thoughts. Pat stared at Ray. "Do you think that buying products with style will become fashionable?"

"Pat, Sergio, buying stylish products has always been fashionable with the few. Our job is to attract the masses."

Sergio first looked at Pat then at Ray. "The way you put it, we only need to dress those few with our creations, and then have the media, if not they themselves, show and tell. Are those your thoughts, Ray?"

"That's right! We'll show and tell them through every billboard and television show money can buy. And do you want to know why I am so fired up? Because that's your job, and I'm sure you two will do just fine."

At twenty-eight, Ray made the sale of his life. Pat and Sergio were becoming his best associates to drive Giglio to the top.

Pat stood up, nodded a few times, and pounded on the table. "You know what, this plan will work. Just words and images associated with who's who will do. I tell you it will. I can see those ads already."

"What do you think, Sergio?"

"It's the way it has to go, Ray. Madison Avenue's experts make that happen every hour of the day a thousand times over. I believe what Pat sees: a mixture of direct and subliminal messages through ads."

"I'm glad you two agree. But always remember; never get cute with words unless you intend to deliver on them. If you do, you'll be right back where you started from, or worse. You can't fool customers with hollow jingles; they have a funny way of getting even, trust me."

The trio got back to the business of taking Giglio to the top.

Sergio wore his controller's hat now. "To get it clear, based on the theory we've talked about, Giglio will expand its operations despite forecasts of bad times ahead?"

Ray looked at the two of them. "That's the spirit."

Pat looked at Ray and smiled. "I'm on board. Where do we start?"

Sergio got up to stretch his legs. He looked around the room then at Ray. "Is Silvana on board?"

"I'm glad you brought that up. As with all creative people, they lose interest when they can't extend their talent to the fullest. Although she's involved in the business, she's an artist first and the business cannot afford to lose her talent."

Pat nodded and so did Sergio as they headed for the break room.

Refreshed and eager to start again, they sat down for another session with Sergio leading.

"Pat, Ray, now that we agreed on how to expand the company, I would like to bring up a subject of interest to us all. As we all know, the road to the top can get bumpy. So I have thought of a way to smooth it out beforehand. It deals with our decision-making processes. From now on, we will hold our meetings in this room twice a week—Tuesdays and Thursdays. In between meetings, we must refrain from discussing any pending topics between ourselves.

"I know what you guys are thinking. But I've discovered that when I'm faced with a tricky question, I get a better answer if I sleep on it for a night of two. When I act hastily, it costs me, at times dearly. So relax. As decision makers, the company deserves the best from us. That is clear, calculated, and unrestrained decisions."

Called away, Ray excused himself for a few minutes.

"I hate to admit it, Sergio, but the man is right."

"I know he is. Since I was a teenager, whenever I'm confronted with a tough question, within a couple of days my brain dishes out the best answer. The funny thing is that I never know when it will pop up, but it always does and when I least expect. It rarely comes to me whole, or in logical sequence, but scrambled, in the order in which I first registered my experiences."

"What do you do when you get that magic answer in the middle of night?"

Sergio pointed to his shirt pocket. "You see this? I always carry a pen and a folded sheet of paper. At night they go from here onto the night table."

"I'll bet that's what writers do to record their thoughts and observations the moment they strike."

"By the way, Pat, I didn't know it was so ingrained in Ray. At one time, Silvana referred to his writing passion. His essays attracted a lot of attention back in Sicily."

"So what happened?"

"I don't know, Pat, but for some reason he put his writing career on hold."

As part of his workload, Ray reserved Wednesdays and Fridays for Mafia affairs; Mondays for planning the week ahead; Saturdays and Sundays strictly for family; and, as scheduled, Tuesdays and Thursdays for Giglio.

To fit the new plan, Ray remodeled the offices. The top halves of the two glass doors facing the elevator were each engraved with a lily that filled the pane. On the far wall of the lobby a neon sign read, *Giglio Enterprises*. The décor invited visitors to trust in the future of the business.

He built a conference room to the left of the lobby. It could hold a dozen CEOs and their entourages. Twenty-four red leather chairs encircled the massive mahogany table. The room was equipped with state-of-the-art recording devices. To the right of the lobby, unaltered, stood the so-called "Steam Room." Here they hashed out strategies among themselves.

Ray, Pat, and Sergio worked on a plan to raise venture capital for the 1964–74 budgets. They needed the money to sell to new markets in the States and abroad. Thanks to Silvana's zeal for new creations, Giglio was a jewel of a company, ready to sparkle in its own world.

Ray signed off on the final plan. "Pat, Sergio, I want to remind you that besides commitment and money, what makes a business plan successful are price, quality, and service with price being first. Giglio Enterprises has it all, and more."

Pat was getting things ready for the first meeting with six CEOs of apparel manufacturers. To bring them on board, he met with scores of contractors. He also arranged for the shooting of several commercials and a dozen printed ads.

Pat was thirty-two and a handsome man of medium height. He had blond hair, blue eyes, and a short jaw line. Thanks to his boyish smile, he did not look a day over twenty-two. His upbeat speech and candid charm made him a great negotiator and a smooth part-time lover. A Harvard graduate, he was most confident at his job when he dressed casually.

The clock ticked toward one, and Sergio was still checking the business plan. Sergio, general manager, was pushing thirty and tall and slim. He was the kind of executive corporate America relished: a Yale graduate dressed in a perfectly tailored dark blue suit. He wore a crisp white shirt and a dark striped tie that matched his black hair. His slim body said, "I'm here for the long run, no matter what." Contrary to his body language, his granite face, brown eyes, and slanted smile revealed nothing he didn't want you to know.

Gabriella, the receptionist, welcomed everyone into the conference room. At one o'clock, Ray and Silvana entered the room.

A large screen on the wall showed a sensuous couple holding hands on a breezy Irish hillside in springtime. They were dressed in clothes of a style never seen before. It was the latest haute couture collection designed by Silvana. At the bottom of the screen, a single line read, "Giglio, the Future and Beyond."

The business plan was to create and promote clothing from casual to formal and sportswear for men and women as well as accessories such as wristwatches, chains, rings, and earrings. Other items were shoes, purses, belts, wallets, luggage, and briefcases.

To fund the advertising budget, the investors would get a ten-year exclusive right to produce Giglio's products at a preset markup over cost. Pat explained the advantages in hiring untainted spokespersons, Sergio outlined the economics, and Ray discussed the overall strategy.

The products needed time to resonate with the consumer. With that conceptual timetable, they all agreed to give the company a dynamic look by hiring fresh models rather than overworked celebrities. It was cheaper, too. The meeting went more smoothly than they had expected.

With the last ads to be aired in the fall and scores more to be posted on billboards everywhere, as well as countless worldwide outlets lined up to sell the new merchandise, Giglio's team enticed the six leading manufacturers to invest in the largest fashion campaign ever undertaken. They would fund the company for all the advertising and manufacturing dollars it would need, with other manufacturers scheduled to join in the venture.

With all sorts of papers spread about, the conference table looked like a City Hall records counter, where people eagerly signed on dotted lines without really knowing what they were signing.

Finally, there was the last of the CEOs signing the agreement. "Mr. Greco, I want you to know that on Mr. Cremona's assurance alone—"

"Excuse me, Mr. who?"

"Mr. Saverio Cremona, of course. As I was saying, all of us were very much ready to go along with your deal even though we thought it was bloody risk. After today's presentation, we feel very confident in your ability to lead the company. I'll see that he knows. You're a bunch of brave lads. . . . I'm sure our venture will be profitable."

After each CEO filed out, nodding and shaking hands, Pat and Sergio retreated to their offices.

Ray and Silvana stared at each other speechless. "Can you imagine his audacity? Under the guise of legal money, your father just secured himself a nice fat deal. And I fell for it! . . . I can't believe I did."

"He's a clever man, Ray. Guess what just dawned on me? He gets a cut from his two brothers' businesses, too. The funny part is they don't even know it. I believe that greed wipes every bit of decency out of a man. You're right, it's incredible, but I don't think he means any harm."

Ray discounted her last sentence as past incidents rushed through his mind. *"Tonight I've settled the score with my brother." "Trust nobody . . . not even me." "Look for a man named Santo when you get to Brooklyn."* Then there was Stefano and Gloria calling for help; Benito Campo and Carlo; and Santo again; and many others. At this moment, the only thing he was certain of was that Don Saverio was using him as a pawn in a game he didn't know existed. He wished he could just walk away. For all he knew, Don Saverio could have owned all the six companies that just invested in Giglio and financed the entire deal himself.

Suddenly, Ray realized why Don Saverio had earmarked those six companies "must call first" on the list of prospects. Painful as it was for Ray, he had to admit Don Saverio was no longer the man aiming at reforming Mafia. To him, Don Saverio became a greedy business tycoon no different from the world's worst or the other heads of Mafia he claimed to despise. Still angry, he ventured to think that Don Saverio might have shielded himself by placing a ten-year financial grip on the company.

Analyzing what he knew, at first Ray thought that it was greed. What made him uneasy, though, was that every time he thought greed, his inner voice told him he was wrong. The apparent facts subdued that voice, taking him into a never-ending cycle of speculation. Disappointed as he was when he first doubted his father's accident, and feeling betrayed, Ray now understood Don Saverio's secret meetings back in Sicily.

To escape the world of Mafia for a while, Don Saverio would allow his business associates to address him as Mister, but only behind closed doors. And also behind closed doors, Don Saverio conceived the plan Ray was yet to discover.

Disillusioned, Ray and Silvana needed time alone to sort things out.

Silvana called on Sergio and Pat to walk her to the train station. She arrived at Montauk Point before nightfall.

Late Saturday afternoon, two days after the meeting, Ray caught up with Silvana. He had thought the entire deal over, and for the moment, he settled for the most favorable solution. It's business, and as long as it stays that way, I must treat it just as ordinary dog-eat-dog business and get on with life. His biggest challenge for now was to comfort Silvana and get her career back on track as well as holding her to her mother-to-be promise.

They sat at the dinner table. Arms crossed, she stared at a bowl of fruit.

"Silvana, I've thought the whole thing over."

"I didn't; it stinks!"

"Look at me, please . . . thank you. I know it stinks, but we have to look to the future. Regardless of whose funds they are, the entire marketing plan revolves around your creations and my know-how to lead the company, not on some baseless scam."

She nodded.

"I had Joel Kaufman look at the agreements, and everything is proper and legal."

"I've no problem with your thinking, Ray, but why?"

"Tradition."

"I don't think so, but if you say so."

"Look at it this way. Investors always put some form of a strong hold on the company they invest in, at least until they get their money back. That's the nature of things. What's hurtful to us is that your father put the squeeze on us with a smile and behind our backs."

She snapped off a small cluster of red grapes. "Why did he? I tell you, Ray, he has something else up his sleeve. And whether we like it or not, someday we'll pay for it."

"Whatever the case, don't forget who controls the company. People are buying your creations, giving you their stamp of approval, not your father. The way I see it, if we are good at what we do, we can always raise money. So relax, let me worry about the financial scheme."

"Didn't we make a deal with my father just before Carlo was killed?"

"Yes. You and I own and manage the company with no strings attached. Carlo would get all other enterprises. If we need money, we'll ask them. They get twenty-five percent of the profits, and we keep the rest. Otherwise, hands off."

"That's all well and good, Ray. I am sure he'll never go back on the numbers. What bothers me, though, is why did he renege on being hands-off? But again, that might be trivial in the scheme of things. But I don't think so." She got up and cleared the table.

Ray's latest revelation was that for Don Saverio to prevent any reprisal, he had cleverly put a ten-year insurance policy on his life by controlling the finances. If he vanished, so would the investors. Aware of that predicament, Ray had to deal with the reality that even if Santo showed Don Saverio to be guilty, he would have to let it pass for the sake of the company, Silvana, and his future family.

Don Saverio had indeed bought himself at least ten years' grace. A time, Ray thought, he would spend weakening Don Saverio's power base.

16

WITH GIGLIO'S BUSINESS PLAN PUT INTO ACTION, Ray had to get things moving if he was to get Santo before the traditional August 31st. With that in mind, he secured the building permit to alter his house at Harman Street and scheduled Sal's return to Brooklyn. This time Sal could not stay at Harman Street, as there would be only one bedroom available. Ray used it for Friday night stopovers on his way to Montauk Point. The people from the ready-mixed concrete plant Sal was visiting offered him a place to stay in Queens. Sal had an innate suspicion regarding hotel registers, so he gladly took up the offer.

Watching through the airplane window, Sal sensed the asphyxiating smog hovering over the city, wondering why people would live in such a climate. On the final approach to runway thirteen-right, the metallic voice of the captain came through the loudspeakers. "Welcome to JFK International Airport. The New York weather is hot and humid, in the upper nineties."

Sal went through customs, then he directed a cab to a diner just east of the airport. At the end of the short ride, he tapped the cabdriver's shoulder with a twenty-dollar bill folded lengthways. Pointing at a parking space, he asked the man to wait for a short while.

Since Ray left Sicily, the hunt for Santo had been Ray's top priority. With the exception of Sal, no one else was privy to his plan, since he worked alone.

Sal walked two cars over and slid into the front seat next to Ray.

"How was the flight?"

"The flight was okay. What worries me is the smog. How the hell you guys take it is beyond me."

"You'll get used to it. Besides, this is a smog-free car," Ray turned the air to max. Built-in air conditioners in automobiles were becoming indispensable add-ons.

"How's Don Nardo?"

Sal squared himself in the seat and labored to loosen his collar. "These damned ties . . . Don Nardo, as you said, a piece of cake. With him money talks. He sent word to Don Mario already. I'm meeting him the day after tomorrow."

"That's good."

Ray handed him a fat envelope. "Here are five ten-thousand dollar bundles and the key to my apartment. Don't forget now, Don Mario knows Santo as Mickey Argento, 'the Cat'. If you call him Santo, you'll give away the store. He might suggest someone else. Just work him until he sets you up with Mickey."

"How much you think he'll take?"

"I hear his luck at poker hasn't been good lately. You have enough money there. But don't let money hold us back. If you've got to, use that as a down payment. Let him collect the balance. Go for it. Don't forget; set the deal up our way."

"For when?"

"Friday night, August 28."

"Just about the end of the month, very traditional. When will I see you?"

"Stop worrying. I'll be okay. . . . . I tell you what I'll do. Saturday morning I'll pick you up, and we'll spend the weekend together at Montauk Point. How's that?

"Silvana would love to see you. In the meantime, let's stay out of each other's way until this is over. Just call me on the phone."

Ray looked at his wristwatch as if to say let's go to work. They got out of the car, Ray walked toward the diner and Sal to the waiting cab.

Getting Don Mario to call Mickey proved to be more expensive than Sal thought. For the privilege of holding back the name of the marked man, Don Mario was getting an extra five thousand. Mickey's price was based on how risky the mission was. With both parties prepped, Don Mario set the meeting for Monday, August 17, at 3 p.m.

Mickey was playing solitaire in the back room. As the time drew near, the tension among the few members in the club was mounting. At three, Sal walked in firing friendly glances around. Without much fanfare, Don Mario led him to Mickey, who sat at the only illuminated table.

They didn't shake hands but acknowledged each other's presence. Sal sat facing him squarely. Mickey looked down at the cards. After Don Mario shut the door behind him, Mickey stopped playing and fixed his eyes on Sal.

Sal didn't flinch.

Mickey narrowed his eyes. "I understand you want to hire me."

"To be precise, it's not me who wants to hire you, but an old friend, Don Saverio Cremona."

Mickey sat back for a moment. "What happened to Carlo? Why didn't he send for me?"

Sal placed a bundle of hundred dollar bills on the table. Then he watched Mickey's composure crumble.

"The reason I'm here, my friend, is because Carlo is dead.

"He got killed last year. Don Saverio wants revenge, and because he doesn't want to alert anyone in the family, he wants you to make the hit. Until the smoke clears, he wants you to deal with me. If we strike a deal, Don Mario knows how to get in touch with me."

"How much is there?"

"Thirty thousand."

"I move no finger for less than fifty. Who's the guy anyhow?"

"His son-in-law, Ray Greco."

"You're joking. Luciano's son?"

"Am I laughing? . . . Did you know Luciano?"

Mickey was in thought. "No, not really, Sal, but I delivered that contract on time and clean, or he wouldn't be looking to hire me again.

"How did he become his son-in-law?"

Sal had linked Mickey to Don Saverio on the first go round. He put the money back in his coat packet and pushed himself off the table. "Mickey, I'm here to buy a contract. I don't ask why or how things happen in life. They're bound to happen in spite of my asking."

Mickey looked at Sal, willing him to stay put. "Don't be so hasty. For old time's sake, I'll do it for forty. Give me the scoop."

"Okay, only if you do it our way."

"You got a deal; thirty thousand now, the rest on delivery."

Sal stared at Mickey for a long moment; then, placed the money back on the table. "When you learn the whereabouts of the hit, you'll agree that this job is as easy as walking out of a poker game to win a couple of sure hands and then back home to win some more."

"In my business, nothing is easy. Just give me the scoop. I worry about the rest."

"I don't mean to teach you the business, but this job has no leeway."

Mickey kept an eye on the money. "Go ahead. I'm all ears."

"On Harman Street, a few blocks from here, Ray has an apartment in a three-family house he owns. Since he started remodeling two of the apartments, every Friday night he pulls in at ten o'clock and he's sound asleep by eleven. Monday through Friday, he runs his business in Manhattan. On Friday nights, he uses this place as a stopover on his way to Montauk Point. He wakes up early Saturday morning, goes over the work, pays the contractors, and takes off for Long Island."

"With a house in Montauk Point and a place in Manhattan, why is he screwing around with a dump?"

"Maybe for sentimental reasons, maybe for business, I ask no questions nor do I set the rules. Don Saverio does that, and here they are:

"The hit has to take place on Friday night in Ray's bedroom, and he has to be found with his cock stuck deep in his throat."

Sal pushed the money toward Mickey. "Don Saverio told me you're a good butcher."

"Why the cock?"

"From what I gathered, besides causing Carlo's death, Ray has been cheating on his wife. You know, Don Saverio's daughter. You know what I mean."

Mickey fanned the money with his thumb. "Okay. I got the idea now. What else you got for me?"

"This is the master key to the front door, his apartment, and the other two apartments. To be safe, you should get there after midnight. If you think to sneak in ahead of time and wait in one of those apartments, you'll spoil the party. He checks them both before he goes to sleep. By the way, I'm told he's a heavy sleeper. And as I said, there is no leeway on this job. A plus, on Harman Street they roll up the sidewalks by nine o'clock."

"I know what you mean. I'll check the place out tomorrow or Wednesday. If there's a problem, Don Mario will call you. Otherwise, Friday will be it.

"By the way, how do I know he's there?"

"He drives a new Olds '98; it'll be the only one on the block. I'll have the other ten waiting for you here on Saturday."

It was Friday. A construction dumpster with a square chute hanging off the second floor window occupied the front yard. It blocked the side door and the two ground floor windows entirely. There was a six-foot hole in the wooden floor. That's where the spiral staircase used to be. A temporary ladder led to the concrete floor below. Ray had tested two ten-foot round nets stronger than those used to catch live bait. He also checked the ropes and pulleys and the intrusion alarm. Then he stored the whole thing in the apartment. In fact, he spent most of last week planning and arranging things.

The kid assured him that a man with silvery hair and a missing finger, holding an official-looking pad, checked the house. Then he went into a hallway three houses down and popped up on the roof where he stood watching things for a while. Maybe making an inspection, the kid thought.

Taking into account his poker game schedule, and operating on the notion that Mickey would follow instructions and not strike before midnight, Ray approached the house at ten without hesitation. For the first time, he realized how quiet the street really was at that time of night. Resolute, he went up the stoop and into the house. With one hour to go before he shut off the lights, Ray checked the second floor and got to work.

He laid the two round nets on top of each other and threaded them together around the edge with a half-inch rope. With a pull on the rope, the nets would turn into a two-ply cocoon capable of holding a man immobile. The ropes were connected to pulleys fastened a few inches from the edge of the hole.

Ray stretched the nets halfway across the room and laid a light-weight carpet over them. He climbed down through the half-open hole and removed the ladder. Standing on a chair and stretching, he slid the trap the rest of the way and made up the ropes. With the trap in place and the alarm set, Ray sat in an armchair facing a light bulb that would flash red the instant the main door opened upstairs.

At five to eleven, he shut the lights off and, like a fisherman waiting for a bite, stood by quietly in the dark.

At three, the light bulb started to flash red. A few minutes earlier, Ray had fallen asleep. Like a cat, Santo came down the hatch and the stairs and into the apartment. He took only two steps before he fell into the trap and banged his head on the floor. The thump, although loud, didn't wake Ray.

Dangling from the ceiling, Santo had cocooned himself into a fetal position. With each attempt he made to free himself, the red light flashed faster, or so it seemed.

The more Santo moved, the tighter the cocoon became. It was almost impossible for him to move a muscle. Realizing the spot he was in, Santo quieted down. He inched his right hand toward the six-inch blade holstered on his ankle. But before he could pull it, a wedge of light shone from the kitchen door. It illuminated the scene just enough for him to see Sal rush in, take the gun from Ray's lap, and disappear from view.

Santo dangled like a pear from a tree. Feeling Sal's breath on his neck, he could only wonder what Sal was up to. When he felt a nylon string around his neck, he wondered no more. Sal pulled hard, very hard in fact, until Santo jolted, causing a key chained to a silver dollar to fall onto the floor. The shrill sound woke Ray just in time to see Sal letting go of Santo's slumped body.

Ray jumped to his feet. "It worked!" Then composed, embarrassed, and relieved all at once, he picked the key up off the floor and looked up. "Sal? . . . Where the hell did you come from?"

There wasn't much discussion amid their urgency to get things ready. The service truck would take the dumpster away at the crack of dawn.

They hoisted the cocoon onto the first floor, stripped Santo of any identification, wrapped him in the carpet, hauled him to the second floor, and sent him down the chute. Then, like common laborers, they filled the dumpster to the brim with debris from the apartments. On his way to help fill a pit in South Brooklyn, Santo was no more.

On their way to Montauk Point, Sal and Ray checked into a motel next to the airport for a couple of hours. They were more exhausted from filling the dumpster than getting rid of Santo.

Rested, in the early afternoon, they went to a diner. During the meal, they only exchanged subtle smiles, praising each other for a job well done. Ray was the first to speak. "I would've loved to squeeze the truth out of him. Why didn't you wake me up?"

"Why? I had him linked to Don Saverio already. Besides, why don't you ask me?"

"I'm not going through this for fun. I want to know why they killed my father."

"First of all, Santo did not know the motive. Ray you know better . . . hit men never do, nor do they care. Look what we told him about you.

"Anyhow, last time out, your grandfather told me that he was told Don Saverio wanted a public road your father was building rerouted to a worthless piece of property he owned. When your father refused because it would have placed an unjust burden on the city's budget, he made the hit list.

"Ray, that's the way they thought in those days."

"For God's sakes, why didn't you guys tell me?"

"Calm down, Ray. Being from the old school, your grandfather thought the revenge had to come from within you. Besides, you still would have to get rid of Don Saverio. The way you were carrying on with him back in Alcamo, your grandfather telling you without sure facts or knowing Santo's whereabouts, not to mention his sour relationship with your mother, he felt it could've had a reverse effect on you. So, he thought the facts were there for you to find, as you ultimately did. Don't ask me how, but he also knew that you were the one to make things right for everyone."

Ray took it in the guts. He had given up his career to avenge his father and make things right, but he had failed to achieve that task yet. He poured cream and sugar in his cup and stirred it slowly for a while, thinking.

"When you see Grandpa, hug him for me, and . . . I owe you one, Sal."

"What about Don Saverio?"

"I would love to jump on the next flight out and revoke his birth certificate myself, but I have to stay put."

"Why?"

"He's still too powerful and too much part of my life. He just bought himself a ten-year life insurance. I have to find a way to revoke that first. For now, it's one down and one to go."

Sal nodded, without knowing what life insurance Ray was talking about.

"Now tell me. How did you get in, and where were you hiding last night?"

Sal reached for his cup and smiled. "Don't forget, Ray, last April your mother and I lived there for a while. Before I gave Santo the key, I made a duplicate. Last night I got there at about eight. I surveyed the place, went downstairs, and read *Il Progresso* for a while. Then I laid a bunch of blankets on the floor, went to sleep, and woke up at two, the time I figured Mickey would show up. I was reading the rest of the paper when I heard a thump. I waited. When I heard nothing else, I came out. Sure enough, there he was dangling off the dining room ceiling."

"Where downstairs?"

"Where else? In your beloved kitchen under the table. Even if you stuck your head in, you couldn't have seen me."

"You know, it never fails. Every time I set an alarm, my mind blanks out and I sleep until the bell rings. Last night there was no bell, just a stupid flashing light. I fell asleep, and I didn't wake up until it was over. I'm sure glad you were there."

"A four-hour wait, especially in the dark, that's a long haul for anybody. But like they say, it's water under the bridge."

"Were you out there one day last week?"

"I was."

"How come the kid didn't tell me?"

"I told you already. I lived there, and I was no stranger to the kid. Besides, I paid him a buck more than you did."

"That little double-crossing son of a bitch, I'll get him!"

17

COMPARED TO THE MORNING SESSION he had with two heads of Mafia, the afternoon was calm and quiet. Ray studied Giglio's financial report. It exceeded all expectations. Before he could pat himself on the back, Gabriella's voice came over the intercom. "Mr. Catania is here to see you."

"Who?"

"Mr. Vito Catania. He says he's an old friend of yours."

"Hold on!"

Stunned, he didn't know what to make of it. He wasn't concerned about Mr. Catania's visit, but wondered how he had found him. After all, the Catanias were as remote from the world of fashion as he was from falling in love with their daughter. I'll bet he doesn't know I got married. That's it! I'd better clear the air.

"Gabriella, please tell Mr. Catania I'll be right out."

Some people never give up. He polished his wedding band as he walked down the hallway.

In the lobby, Ray faced a short-legged man. He looked different from the man he knew. This one was bald. He was squeezed into a three-piece suit like a salami. His collar was so tight that his face changed color with each breath he took. Ray could not deny that the man was indeed Mr. Catania. He reached for his hand. "How are you?"

Mr. Catania forced a constipated smile. Gabriella clasped her hand over her mouth to muffle her giggles, but her eyes betrayed her. Ray led Mr. Catania to his office and pointed to a chair next to his desk.

"Please have a seat, Mr. Catania."

Mr. Catania sat and loosened his collar. "Don Greco . . . I need your help . . . badly."

"Hold on! Before we go any further, let's get something straight. I'm not, nor do I wish to be a 'Don'. Please don't."

"I'm sorry. I didn't mean to offend you. But I need help."

"I don't know what I can do for you."

Mr. Catania wiped sweat off his forehead with a soggy handkerchief.

"Plenty, Mr. Greco . . . plenty."

Under Ray's sympathetic eye, Mr. Catania poured out his whole story. "Concetta, my little Concetta, is lying in bed staring at the ceiling for over a week now. She . . . she was raped. The church's new groundskeeper, he was working there less than a month. The cops are saying it was consensual . . . they won't do a thing. Here's his picture. The son of a bitch lives alone in a shack behind the church, two blocks from where Concetta works. If you look at him, he laughs in your face for spite. He's bad, very bad. I know you can; you've got to help. Please do something, please."

Ray poured him a glass of water.

"Mr. Catania, calm down please. Here, relax. Have a drink. Everything will be okay. Relax now."

Ray paused in thought.

Mr. Catania bowed his head.

"Mr. Catania, I'm very sorry for you and your family. My heart goes out to your daughter, but I'm not what you think I am. I am the same guy who took your advice and quit my job to stay away from that sort of thing. I'm sorry, but I can't help you. You need to go to the district attorney or some other law enforcement agency in your district. They're there to help you. Trust me."

Mr. Catania smiled softly, then rose and reached out for Ray's hand.

"Out of curiosity, where did you get the notion that I could help?"

"Mr. Greco, you know, from the first time we met, I've been upfront with you. So allow me to tell you that you've a good friend in Nino Maltese. He's the one who took the picture of the groundskeeper."

Ray was flabbergasted. He hadn't thought of Nino since the days they had gone to the social clubs together.

"Since he got back from Sicily . . . he thinks the world of you. You know he spent five full days there last year. He says you can solve any problem at the snap of a finger."

Ray was somewhat flattered, having not seen or heard from Nino for more than two years. Ray thought to himself: *Five full days? It would take more than a year for people to give a stranger the time of day, let alone a history lesson in who's who.*

"Mr. Catania, I'm surprised at you. I can understand you reaching out for help, but a man of your experience should not listen to a guy like Nino. He thrives on gossip. Trust me. He lives in a world of fantasy, making up Mafia stories."

Ray pulled on his suspenders to reinforce his point. "What's sad is someday he'll get hurt badly . . . but again, that's his problem. Wouldn't you say?"

"Well, if Nino is making it all up, he can get you in some hell of hot water. There's no stopping him when he starts talking. But knowing your grandfather and Don Saverio, it's hard for me to think . . . but let me ask you, is Nino that far off? . . . Is he?"

Ray pulled on his suspenders again.

Mr. Catania got up and wobbled down the corridor with Ray toward the lobby. They stopped, and he held Ray's arm pleading, "Please, help Concetta . . . please."

Back at his desk, Ray looked at the rapist's photo. He picked up the phone and dialed seven digits.

"May I speak with Gregory Khan, please?"

"Hi Greg, Ray here. Uh-huh.

"Okay. Tonight at nine. Uh-huh . . . Harman Street.

"See you."

In the deserted moonlit quarters, the church's cupola shadowed the shack. The rapist's loud snoring came through the corrugated walls of the makeshift bedroom. Greg opened the unlatched door, drew near the man lying on an old four-poster bed, and knocked him out with a single blow to the head. He taped his mouth shut, stripped him naked, and tied him spread-eagle to the four posts.

By the time Greg had smoked a cigarette, the rapist came to. He yanked hard on the ropes to free himself. His troubled face with devil eyes and reddish curly hair did not conceal his age. He wasn't more than twenty.

Greg stared at him blankly, crushing the cigarette butt on the floor. He reached for the jar of Vaseline he had placed on the night table. The rapist looked on in horror.

Greg dipped a nightstick in the Vaseline and covered the tip well. Nonchalantly, he shoved it up the rapist's ass. He turned and twisted it until the rapist's eyes bulged with red tears. To prolong the man's agony, Greg jerked the nightstick up, around, and in and out, like he was digging for gold.

The rapist passed out. When he came to again, Greg pulled out a straight razor and, under the muffled screams of the rapist, with a single stroke, he cut off his balls.

He wiped the razor and the nightstick clean as he stood by, watching the bright eyes glaze over until the rapist was no more.

The following day the media blamed the atrocity on gangland infighting.

At the news, Concetta rejoiced and began to breathe normally again. Mr. Catania also rejoiced. Wisely, he thanked no one.

One evening, several weeks after the rapist was killed, Mr. Catania left the club, contented. Concetta had recovered from the ordeal, and her family was back to normal.

Waiting for the high rollers, Nino ordered a Coke with double rum. He gulped the drink down and quickly ordered another one. He tried to read the paper but could not.

He couldn't help thinking about what Mr. Catania had told him and about how close he was to getting hurt. He looked around to thank

Mr. Catania for his warnings, but he had already gone home. Thinking to himself that he'd talk to him the following day, Nino fell asleep in the recliner. He awoke before the high rollers began to file in. Still feeling the effects of his double rums, he rose and staggered to the street. Somewhat unstable, with slumped shoulders and staring at the sidewalk, he walked toward his car.

He watched his shadow following him. He saw the concrete cracks, the broken curb, the dirty whitewall tires, and the shining hubcaps. He walked with his head down, even when crossing the intersection. On the other side of the street, he kept watching the cracks, the whitewall tires, and the hubcaps, until he recognized his rear bumper.

At the next step, he spotted a pair of black patent leather shoes. He leaned against his car and raised his head slowly. He looked from the shoes to the blue trousers past half a dozen brass buttons to a face with a fake smile. The police officer opened the passenger door and invited Nino into the front seat.

As Nino tried to slide toward the driver's side, he never even heard the sound of the silenced gun go off and the single bullet that entered his skull behind his right ear. Greg allowed the body to slump to the left without triggering the horn. He put the silencer away, shut the door, and resumed his beat.

18

THE SIXTIES AND EARLY SEVENTIES sparked unique social up-heaval. It was far more chaotic than the twenties had been in America. Politics, culture, and mores were uprooted and forever changed as the world watched. People sought their desires and more.

Martin Luther King had a dream. Cities were set afire, and the American flag was placed on the moon. Johnson bowed out of the presidency. Nikita Khrushchev embraced Castro. Cassius Clay, twenty-three, took the title of heavyweight champion of the world from Sonny Liston.

Youth rebelled against military ideology. At the Woodstock Music Festival and Art Fair in Bethel, New York, they openly displayed their strength, appeal, power, and much more. Toward the end of the sixties, Wall Street lost its craving for speculative public offerings. Venture capital was hard to get.

In the midst of it all, Ray Greco quietly managed to carry out his agenda. The best years for Don Saverio's plan were from 1960 to 1973. Along with many other Ivy League graduates, the Class of '56 found jobs as high-ranking staffers. In their positions, they became the brains behind politicians and business leaders alike.

They supplied the backbone every leader needed. Because they were good at what they did, their services were indispensable. There was no stopping them.

As planned, Don Saverio's protégés were infiltrating American politics and big business from within. Meanwhile, Sergio and Pat were expanding Giglio worldwide, and Sal was expanding the gravel business back in Sicily. He was also experimenting with ready-mixed concrete. Silvana reared three children and spent the summers at Montauk Point. The rest of the year she and her family lived in Scarsdale.

On the illegal side, Ray took over Carlo's job of dismantling the remaining Mafia families. With his grandfather's conviction about his father's murder, Ray's already tarnished trust in Don Saverio turned to contempt.

While he wanted to kill Don Saverio at once, Ray controlled the impulse. It would upset the scheme of things. It would also drive the moles to retaliate against him, for their survival was on the line. In the interim, to take advantage of the control he had over the moles and their desire to go back home, Ray set up a plan to weaken Don Saverio's power base.

In keeping with his own plan, Ray didn't accept anything Don Saverio said or did without first checking the facts and consequences himself. His mother's words, "Trust nobody," continued to bring to mind the man who had made the wrong choice, Don Saverio.

Had Don Saverio rejected Ray as stranger's blood, Santo would still be alive and out of Ray's reach. It was that trust that led Don Saverio to put Ray at the helm of the "new enterprises" and now of the moles.

While Ray was much obliged to fate, the past and immediate future held a bitter taste. He restrained himself from killing Don Saverio before it was time.

At the FBI headquarters in Manhattan, special agent John DeMaria was interrogating two members of the Caiello family. While the FBI wanted to dig up enough dirt on these two guys to put them away for life, John wanted more than a conviction. He wanted to increase his record for the most Mafia members turned informers and the most toppled Mafia families. On this occasion, he wanted to add to his list of acclaimed mobsters the elder of the two men, Tony Fraterno.

The two informants were now driving across the Brooklyn Bridge. Joey slowed down to let the traffic through. "You got to do it, Tony! It's you or them, no way out."

Getting out of the morning traffic could be as big a relief as getting off the Caiello family's hit list. Both were deadly. Done with the bridge crossing, Tony and Joey Verona arrived at the downtown diner one hour earlier than scheduled. From there, an FBI agent would take them to their secret destination.

They sat in a corner booth. Joey knocked a pack of Camels in the palm of his hand and nodded a few times. "Look, Tony, you're over sixty, and the only things you've got to show are twenty-four hits and a terrible fear for your life."

Tony looked down in shame. "I know."

"And look at me. I'm forty with six hits of my own, and I'm as scared as you are."

Joey paused to light up a cigarette. "I'm telling you, Tony, we're in some hell of a shit."

"I know."

"The only thing I know is that when loyal men like us are kicked out on their asses on a single suspicion, something's wrong."

"Not even a chance to defend myself, and I even whacked friends and relatives for them. Some hell of a thank you. I tell you, Joey, that ain't right."

Joey blew smoke in his coffee. "The truth is that no matter how you look at it, you and I have been royally screwed."

"Uh-huh."

"If we want to stay alive, we've no other place to turn to, and guess what, Tony? I don't know about you, but one way or another I'm going to survive. I got lots of things to do yet."

"Don't get me wrong, Joey; I hear you loud and clear. Since we talked last, I made up my mind. There are no second thoughts here. I'm going to squeal."

"Then, why are you so down in the dumps? What's your regret?"

"That I didn't slit their throats when I had the chance. Joey, I slaved all my life for both brothers." He wiped a sugar spill off the table as his eyes quivered.

"They were family to me; then, one day you wake up, and your life is over. Your family is your enemy, your friends look the other way, and there is no place to turn." For the first time ever, Tony shed a tear.

He was a large man, baldheaded, with sloping shoulders. Because he was an assassin who struck quickly and left no trail, he had become Caiello's most trusted hit man. And yet, because he knew too much, he was a marked man without friends. Reacting to that truth, he joined the FBI's informant program in exchange for safety. On the other hand, Joey went out of his way to please him. Single-handedly, Joey was destroying one of the most powerful Mafia families. As a mole, he wedged himself between Tommy Caiello and Tony. Now he was driving that wedge all the way through, cracking the family apart. Joey was excited: At last, he was going back home.

It was Friday lunchtime when his private line rang.

"Hi Ray, John here."

"Where are you?"

"Here in Manhattan. How about lunch?"

"Sure, where?"

John DeMaria, a Yale graduate, was the first member of the Class of '56 to join the FBI. He rose to the rank of special investigator. In his thirties, he was credited with dismantling two of the largest Chicago families, the Mannino and the Abbruzzese. His bullet-free tactics became legendary within the bureau.

When John walked into an interrogation, there was no doubt as to who was in charge. He had a muscular build on a six-foot-one frame. His light brown hair was mismatched with his black mustache, which concealed a broad pair of lips. His smile said, "I know all about you." He was a born investigator. His immediate subordinates were two Italians and three Irish. His only boss was Ray.

Lenny's, on the east side of Manhattan, was famous for its juicy prime rib. John would say, "You can bite through a one-inch cut with your lips."

He was having coffee at a corner table when Ray came through the front door. John stood up and waved. Except for getting older, nothing had changed since the time they were growing up in Sicily. As most native Sicilians do, they instinctively sat with their backs to the wall facing all newcomers.

"Hi John, am I late?"

"I just got here."

"I never tried this place."

"Wait till you taste the prime rib."

"John, is this an okay place for us to meet?"

"Why not? All my work revolves around Mafia. As long as I bring in convictions, the only things I can get are citations for bravery."

"And a thanks from Don Saverio," said Ray smiling.

"Ray, these days you'd better look beyond Sicilian Mafia. I learned that in this country; besides Sicilian and Neapolitan, there is a strong Irish Mafia and other nationalities, too."

"I'm aware of that. I also know that most of the Irish families you're talking about are seeds Don Saverio planted back then. They are no different from the one we're planting now. Anyhow, what brought you here?"

Before John could answer, the waiter cut in. "The usual?"

"Sure, make it two."

With the waiter out of the way, John looked around and moved closer to Ray. "I need a clearance on one of Caiello's guys I'm investigating."

"Who?"

"Joey Verona."

"How did you know he belongs to us?"

"He was wearing the Class of '56 pin on his lapel. Is he okay?"

"Absolutely; we placed him there about ten years ago."

"Ten years?"

"Whatever it takes. Tony was a big fish, so Carlo got Joey to work on him."

"Can I use him?"

"That's why he's there. He's sharp. You'll see. Another thing you should know: Caiello gave Joey the contract on Tony for squealing."

"I see."

"The Caiello family is a big catch. They have to go. Call Michael Marchese. You know he's with the IRS now."

"I know."

"Last week I asked him to put together a package on these guys. I'm sure you can use it."

"I'm sure; Michael's a good boy."

"I'm proud of Michael. Until Marco got him in the IRS, I was concerned."

"I see."

"But now he's proved to be valuable. Once the Caiello family falls, the others will follow suit."

"How many people did Marco place in my bureau?"

"Since he got situated on Capitol Hill, he placed lots of people in many bureaus."

"What kind?"

"Remember John. Each year back in Sicily, there are new graduates with the same commitment you and I have, if not stronger. As planned, by the mid-seventies we'll have the run of things here. Trust me."

"Do we have a list?"

"Knowing who they are serves no purpose. What's vital is that these people are out there ready to help at a moment's notice. So let's keep up the good work. We have plenty of work ahead."

John nodded. The aroma of brown gravy, mashed potatoes, and fresh green beans reached the table before the prime rib did. Ray looked at the dish then at John.

"What's next for Joey and Tony?"

"As soon as I place them in the program, which should be late next week, I'll turn the case over for prosecution. Then I'll be free to work on others. Believe me; the chief prosecutor wants this family worse than we do."

"Good, but don't forget. After the trial, I want Tony and Joey's new identities. Ship Tony to the Coast; once he gets there, Joey will take care of him. Then he goes back to Sicily."

While informers found refuge in the FBI program, in it Ray found the tool for weakening Don Saverio. One by one, Ray disposed of every mole Don Saverio had placed in America.

To the surprise of most experts, the prosecution won the trial that had dominated the media for the better part of six months. The Cai-ello brothers, one *sottocapo*, and three *consiglieri* were found guilty. They would spend the rest of their lives behind bars without chance of parole.

These convictions, coupled with the FBI's resolve, did more for the would-be informers than for the next-in-line formidable heads of Mafia. They stubbornly refused to wise up. Informers, either of their own accord or influenced by the events, came forward in droves. This signaled the beginning of the end for old Mafia.

At Leonardo da Vinci Airport, Alitalia was paging Mr. Baldisi. He was hoping to get an earlier flight. Unable to get out and on his way to the restroom, a voice from behind him called, "Joey!"

Not yet trained to respond to the calling of Nick only, he found himself facing Sal Rocca.

"What are you doing here? You should be in Palermo!"

"Ray changed plans. He wants you to lay low here for a while, until things cool down a bit."

"What's so hot?"

"Look, Joey, I was asked to meet you here. You know how it is?"

"So where are we going?"

"I got you a room as Nick Baldisi."

Joey was flabbergasted. "How in hell do you know my new name? It's supposed to be top secret, and here I am starting all over."

"Don't worry. You don't want to hide from Don Saverio and Ray, do you?"

"Don't put words in my mouth, Sal."

They walked down the concourse quietly. Outside the terminal, Sal hailed the first cab in line.

"Don't worry; you're okay. No one knows Nick Baldisi exists."

Thanks to the cabdriver's lead foot, they made it to the Excelsior Hotel in record time. They didn't need a bellboy; Joey was traveling light. The sunlit hotel room faced the Eternal City's most revered site, the Vatican. Joey was still uneasy about the change in plans.

"Are things hot because of Tony? Or is the FBI after my ass already?

"I don't know, Joey."

"I've got to know. When I dumped that idiot, I stripped him of all IDs. Not even his mother could identify him. You know, I spent the better part of ten years pretending."

"Uh-huh."

Joey disrobed for a shower. "Sal, I want to go home and relax a bit."

"You were talking about Tony before, right?"

Stripped naked he nodded. "Right."

"Relax, Joey. Take your shower, rest a little, and I'll pick you up in a couple of hours for dinner. We'll talk then."

Joey squinted in the sunlight. "All right, Sal."

Sal drew the curtains shut. "Maybe you can go home tomorrow. I'll call Ray and see what he says."

Joey walked toward the bathroom. "You know, Sal, I earned my keep. Remind Ray, I'm the one who got rid of the Caiello family. Besides, I got work to do for Don Saverio, and whether he likes it or not, I'm going home tomorr—"

A single bullet entered the back of his skull.

"Welcome home," said Sal. He returned the silenced gun into its holster, collected Joey's ID, and left the room quietly, leaving behind an unknown corpse; there never was a Nick Baldisi.

19

VICTOR COMO WAS ANGRY, resentful, and disappointed. Life had stung him bitterly. He spent five of his twelve years as a marketing consultant on the West Coast. In that time, he had helped many companies grow to their full potential, one of which was Kiesco, Kohaski Import Export and Supply Company, Incorporated.

A retired general, Dan Kohaski founded Kiesco some ten years earlier. It was a brokerage house set up to sell general supplies to the Pentagon. Kiesco also bought and sold Pentagon surpluses. At the time, its customers were other U.S. agencies. On those occasions, Kiesco simply shifted supplies from one agency to another, as if playing chess, moving them from one square to the next. As a brokerage house, it kept no inventory, the very thing Victor fell in love with.

Although Kiesco's earnings were high, its sales volume did not justify the price tag. For the right price, Victor thought of buying two-thirds ownership. This would be effective, provided the General kept his connections committed to the company and his salary and expenses trimmed to the bone.

To drive Kiesco to its full potential, Victor knew he had to use every resource available, so he set up some good window dressing with a strong board of directors.

When all the pieces fit, he signed a letter of intent with a one-hundred-thousand-dollar binder. But just after the General went off on a two-month vacation to Europe, a federal marshal showed up with a subpoena. A committee investigating the Pentagon's procurements had a few questions. A later date with the General's secretary and a closer review of the books quickly justified to Victor the committee's concern. At Ray's insistence, Victor walked away from the deal.

Angelo Sutera picked up Victor and Nora at Bradley Airport in Connecticut and drove them to his home. Angelo, Victor's closest friend, was well connected now in the insurance business. He had asked him to spend the weekend with him. Ray was due back from the 1968 fashion show in London the following Monday.

Lia, a petite young woman with long black hair, was born and raised in Sicily. Judiciously, she spent most of the day preparing a meal for the arriving guests. Like most Sicilians, she let her husband think he was the master of the house. And, like most Sicilian women, she was content with the arrangement.

After dinner, with the excuse of giving the women more breathing space, the two men retired to the studio with coffees in hand. The setting sun was coming through the fluffy clouds, the trees, and the curtains. The picture window showed the beauty of a New England autumn closing down the season with the colors of turning leaves.

To the right of the window, wood was piled up against the wall and a set of black iron spikes stood ready to fuel the fireplace. Victor and Angelo were drawn to the mantelpiece like boys to a candy store window. There was a framed photograph of Angelo, Victor, and Ray in their bathing suits at Alcamo Marina. And there was Don Saverio and his wife and Ray and Silvana on their first date at Sala Arlecchino, with Carlo grinning in disbelief.

The most memorable photograph, though, was that of Victor's date without a chaperon. With the astonished faces of onlookers in the background witnessing the end of an era, Victor walked tall, like a matador, arm-in-arm with Brigitte. Victor need not have been ashamed of his setback in California, for he was safe at home now. Here, in his people's minds, he was a champion. In his hometown not too long ago, he had broken a tradition that no other young man dared attempt. Angelo and Victor stood staring at each other for a short while.

"Angelo . . . I guess you heard."

"I did."

They nodded for a second longer then hugged and patted each other's back.

Angelo eased back. "Victor, we need you here. Are you ready to leave California?"

"I am," he said, taking his seat. "Thank you for the welcome. Ray asked me to meet him Wednesday."

"That's good."

"I tell you, Angelo, what a jackass I was. That son of a bitch stung me . . . and I can't do a damn thing. . . . It hurts."

Angelo shook his head.

Victor, squinting his eyes, watched a couple of squirrels chasing each other up and down a birch tree.

"Do you know, ever since he started in business, he billed Uncle Sam ten, even a hundred times the contracted price?"

"And I'll bet Uncle Sam paid the bill in full every time. How did he get away with it?"

"Easy. Kiesco secured a bunch of contracts for supplies on an 'as needed basis' by underbidding the competition by as much as 20 percent. Once the orders were shipped, using the bill of lading, which showed quantities but no price, they billed Uncle Sam at either ten times or one hundred times the contracted price."

"How's that possible?"

"I told you, easy. . . . There's a method known to thieves like him as the MCE system, where M equals per thousand, C per hundred, and E is each. An item contracted, say, at one hundred dollars per thousand is billed at the same one hundred dollars but per hundred, increasing the invoice tenfold. To increase the value a hundredfold, they just bill that same item at one hundred dollars each."

"I imagine there's a safety hatch?"

"Sure, inside connections. It was all rigged. To get the bids awarded, especially when there was no competition, he would submit two or three complementary bids through fake companies. To support the scam, the inside people made sure that Kiesco's MCE unit prices, as well as those of the competition, were posted properly. Items contract-ed, as I said, at one hundred dollars per thousand were posted at one hundred dollars per hundred, and so on."

"How did you find out?"

"Well, I dated his secretary."

"Uh-huh. Here we go."

"She told me more than I cared to know. There was a plan in place; if caught, they declared the incident a mistake in posting. Blame the clerks and reimburse promptly for the over-billed items."

"How did it turn sour?"

"Greed, some insiders thought they weren't getting enough."

"You did good. Let Ray handle the General."

"People are simply stupid. In a court of law, it's easier to defy a bunch of witnesses accusing you of murder than a single piece of paper accusing you of stealing. The paper trail will get you every time. If you remember, Don Saverio always made a point of that."

"What's the chance for the General getting away with it?"

"It's in his favor. We'll see what Ray has to say. By the way, how's the old man?"

"Ever since he lost Carlo, I hear he lives secluded. But I don't really know much. Ask Ray."

"Do you think Ray took over Carlo's work, too?"

Angelo reached for his coffee. "If he did, he's not telling. Person-ally, I don't think Ray ever wanted any part of Mafia."

"I gathered that much long ago. But putting that aside, who's doing Carlo's work?"

"Good question."

"Maybe Ray . . . maybe the grunts?"

"Victor, if you're referring to Don Saverio's moles, that was never a secret to us. If you remember, he took pride in pointing them out at the farewell party. What's a secret, though, or I should say a mys-tery, is that more than half of the moles are not going back home. Ray thinks that once enrolled in the Witness Protection Program, life gets simpler."

"Sure, I can see that. With new identities and a new start, they simply retire into a world of their own. But what does all this mean to Don Saverio?"

"A very destructive blow. These are Don Saverio's most-trusted people."

"You're right, and I'm concerned, too. However, I don't see how their disappearances hindered our cause in any way. These people did exactly what they were supposed to do—destroy the old Mafia. What happens after is irrelevant."

"I know, but Don Saverio gets hurt."

"I wouldn't worry, Angelo. If I read him right, he has that planned, too. At this stage of the game, he would rather retire than have to deal with any of this. He's no youngster."

They rendezvoused on the tarmac of Westchester County Airport. Aunt Laura, who had spent the whole day cooking, got there before everybody else. She took little Luciano, Francesca, and Saverio, but left the dog home. The grownups, Victor, Nora, Angelo, and Lia, got there just in time.

Little Luciano loved to watch airplanes landing. Like his dad, he had an imagination of his own. Fast approaching from the north, the jet crossed the fence line. Its wheels smoked and engines roared as if refusing to slow down. It was that loud roar of the engines followed by the steady hissing that led little Luciano to imagine the jet as a big wildcat prowling through the sky brought down by man to purr like a kitten.

Before they left London, Silvana asked Aunt Laura to put out a good Sunday dinner even though it was Monday. She wanted to celebrate Giglio's fashion show. They were also hungry for a homemade meal and good company.

Aunt Laura never married. Besides being an embroiderer, she was a good cook. After closing down her needle shop in Sicily, she took up the challenge of helping Ray and Silvana out with the children and cooking. In her late fifties, heavyset and gray-haired now, she had a warm, smiling, and guileless face and a faint mustache.

As the two limousines pulled into the driveway, Rex barked as the maid went to the front door. The aroma of fresh-cooked food was as enticing as the table setting. Besides the meatballs and fried zucchinis, there was the main course: linguini with sautéed chopped lamb. It was made with onions, parsley, other spices, and a touch of wine simmered into a thick meat sauce, Aunt Laura's specialty. It was a delicacy whose outcome rested with the skill of the cook. Breaded veal cutlets, eggplants, dried codfish, chicken cacciatore, and sausage with peppers and onions were add-ons to the main course. A bowl of sliced steamed carrots in olive oil, garlic, and parsley was for the diehards. Seasoned black olives in oil and garlic, stalks of white celery, and a spread of fresh fruit were provided to help the meal go down.

Then, looking around for more food to put out, Aunt Laura thought again. *What kind of dinner would it be without a few slices of prosciutto, provolone, and pecorino and, of course, breads and white and red wines? What are they going to think of me?*

The "Sunday" afternoon ended with espresso, *cannolis*, and a long nap to boot. *Aunt Laura knows how to cook*, thought the children. It wasn't until nine that night that Ray, Victor, and Angelo were in any condition to gather in the studio. As further punishment, Aunt Laura placed fresh coffee, a tray of vanilla biscuits, and a bottle of sambuca on the serving table. The trio settled down in their chairs.

"You lucky stiff, Ray."

"She's family, Victor. She loves Silvana and the children as her own."

"How old are they now?"

"Five, four, and two, give or take a month."

"So far their namesakes paid off everyone but Donna Maria. You better get busy."

"No more."

"Why?"

"It's a personal choice. Anyhow, how did you do with the General?"

"As you advised, I walked away."

"Good." Then, he looked at Angelo, "How much so far?"

"Little over two hundred and sixty-five thousand."

"It's all from your line of credit, right?"

"Right."

"Victor, do you think the General can pay it back?"

"From what I know, only if we keep him in business. As long as that subpoena is out there, he's not coming back. He's done this before and gotten away."

"We'll see. Do you have his address in Europe?"

"Sure." Victor jotted it down on a pad.

"You're not going to—"

"Come on! Give me some credit, Angelo. For God's sakes, I'm not going to risk it all over him. Besides, if push comes to shove, we have enough clout with the FBI, IRS, other agencies, and the media to put Kiesco and hundreds more like it out of business without lifting a finger."

"You're right. . . . Sorry I asked."

"By the way, tomorrow I'll have Sergio send you a check to pay off the line of credit. As for the General, if we lose the money, so be it."

Ray reminded Victor of their meeting Wednesday afternoon.

Giglio occupied the entire forty-second floor. Gabriella had become Ray's personal secretary. Ray was now thirty-six, and without a day of working out, he still had an enviable build.

A large octagonal table was set at the center of the steam room. It had a solid tabletop. Each side formed a workstation with a high-backed swivel chair, a telephone, and a nametag. So far, only four engraved nametags—Ray, Silvana, Sergio, and Pat—were in place. The other four stations were for advisors or friends. On Tuesdays and Thursdays, the room turned into a strategic center.

By 2 p.m. their creative talent energized the room. Their success was reflected in the pinups on the walls, now familiar to the world. This room was Giglio's private Hall of Fame. Success was truly in the air. The dynamics of the setup overcame all guests. On this day, only the foursome was present. Silvana opened the meeting.

"Look, guys, the fact that we won more favorable reviews for the fall than the winter collections only shows that in this business we must never let down our guard, if we want to become the kind of pacesetters we're hoping to be."

Ray seconded her.

"We might spend a decade introducing must-have items for the in-vogue, but the facts are that if we fail to keep a finger on the pulse of the consumer, we could lose it all in a single season."

Pat narrowed his eye a bit. "Silvana, at a time when middle-class America is vocal about values, I think you have to tone down your creations a bit. And I'm not talking about miniskirts for girls, even though you should add back an inch or two. I'm talking about dresses for women who are not yet ready for clothes that invite attention."

"What are you talking about?"

"Plain and simple, Sergio. If Middle America, the so-called silent majority, is not ready, they will see our creations as crude and sexually aggressive. In the future, the romance trend might find its audience. For now, I don't think these dresses are possible."

"But why?"

"Can't you see? The present trend favors clothes that serve as day-wear as well as eveningwear; sexual equality is much further down the road than we think."

"Silvana, what Pat is saying is that we're getting ahead of the times."

She looked at Ray unconvinced.

"Do you remember what happened to the Edsel? Although it was a stylish car, the Edsel vanished quickly. Its design was a couple of years ahead of its time. Besides dresses, we have to worry about an array of products that bear our label."

She did not argue with Ray, but took it in stride.

In these meetings, no one took offense; nor were there defeats. Expanding on useful criticism was their formula for success. In that spirit, the first round of debate on what styles to send to the next show took up most of the afternoon. Silvana and Pat found a middle ground on skirt length and female attire. Silvana agreed to wait a few years before letting loose what she had in store for women.

Sergio leaned back on his chair and looked around the table. "I believe we've hammered this subject long enough. As we all know, we've got new collections in stock that cover styles from now to the year 2000 and beyond. With due respect to Silvana here, that tells me not to worry about creations for the near future."

"What worries me," Pat cut in, "and it should worry you, too, is venturing into the future without a solid production team."

Ray looked on across the table. "I know, if you're talking about those dragging us down, the only good news is that their contracts end a year from now. No, Sergio, you don't have to say a word. We all know they've provided the bulk of monies, but that's done and over. We got ours; they got theirs and much more. What we need to do is to replace them quietly, one by one, within the next six months."

Pat shuffled three sheets of paper in his hands. "Do you know what bothers me? The more money these bastards are making, the more they drag their feet. As if they want us out of business. . . . Am I the only one to sense this?"

There were no takers.

Pat tossed the paper into the center of the table. "I prepared this short list; I thought it might fit the bill."

Ray reviewed them on the fly. "To you, it might be a short list. When we decide to switch, you sure have some hell of traveling to do."

"Whatever it takes."

Ray smiled. "You're a good peddler, Pat. For now, let's sleep on it for a couple of days. In the meantime, I see no harm in digging a little deeper into these new guys. At first glance, they seem okay.

"One more thing: Let me assure you that Silvana and I are more anxious than you are to get things back on track.

"Pat, I think you can use some help. I'm meeting Victor tomorrow. He's in between deals. If you want, I'll ask him. He can be of great help to you."

"I sure hope so; I like Victor a lot."

After dinner, with Rex in the doghouse and the children fast asleep, Ray and Silvana discussed the day's events. It was a custom they cherished, meeting either by the bedroom porch or by the fireplace on cooler nights. Tonight, the autumn weather kept them indoors.

"Do you still think my father—"

"He already has."

"You're right. I just can't accept it."

"Since your brother was killed and most of the moles disappeared, he feels threatened by anything that moves."

Ray poked the top log into the flames. "To feel safe, he has to call the shots."

"I'm glad you didn't forget, but there are things he cannot do through business connections alone."

The evening progressed into night. Silvana poked the stubborn log a few times.

"Maybe, if I had a face-to-face talk with him."

"Wake up to reality, Silvana. We started that way. Remember Stefano? To him family comes second. Besides, you're no longer daddy's little girl."

"I guess I got lucky."

"I know you did."

"Well, that stands to reason."

"That's why we must stand by our convictions the same way he does, no matter what."

"By the way, what's up with the General?"

Ray got up to poke the log himself. "Don't dodge the question."

"What about the General?"

"Is he going to get away with it?"

"Do you know what's wrong with this log? It's damp . . . John put a tail on him. And, contrary to what Victor thinks, he can pay. He's unleashing a bag of tricks with a woman. He's living on a million dollars in a fat bank account in Switzerland."

They headed for the bedroom as the fire leapt, throwing their shadows on the wall. The dry log crackled and snapped, spitting sparks in an effort to regenerate.

20

WEDNESDAY MORNING AT TEN FIFTEEN, Ray got off the elevator full of energy. In the lobby, there were two men dressed casually
and another in a business suit looking at Ray in wonder.

"Good morning," Ray said. He walked to his office and reached for
the intercom. "Gabriella, who are those guys?"

"They're your eleven o'clock appointment, Joel's party."

"Thanks."

Valuing Ray's business judgment, Joel Kaufman, his accountant,
had asked him to look into a business deal Sol Katz, a friend of friend,
was proposing. Joel had asked Ray to pay special attention to Sol. He
seemed to know a little too much about the ins and outs of the stock
market. At eleven o'clock, Gabriella led the group into Ray's office.
Ray got up as Sol and the others approached.

"We got here sooner than we thought. My name is Sol Katz, pleased
to meet you, Mr. Greco. Allow me to introduce Nick Amato, president, and Carmine Rizzo, secretary and treasurer of Research Unlimited, Inc."

Ray shook hands with the three men and waved them to their seats.
Carmine and Nick took the sofa, Sol and Ray the chairs at the opposite
ends of the coffee table.

"Joel tells me you have an interesting proposal."

"I think we do."

"Well, let's hear it."

Nick wrung his hands then looked at Ray. "Mr. Greco, Carmine and I have worked long and hard at researching this plan. Now we only need some seed money to make it work. You can triple your investment in less than a year, plus a ten thousand share option at a buck each."

Ray looked at Nick dumbfound.

Nick, mistaking Ray's look, became more enthused. To make matters worse, Carmine cut in. "You can't get a better deal nowhere else."

"For God's sake, Carmine, he knows that."

Nick looked at Ray. "Mr. Greco, I'm sorry for his interruption. I got the idea from a new issue that was offered six months ago. This scientist wanted to make a prototype of his invention. On that alone, they took him public for over a million. If it weren't for a bunch of pros like Mr. Katz here and some seed money, the company would've never gone public. Now it owns all sorts of parking lots across the city. And guess what, its officers are getting good salaries and benefits, too."

"What's a scientist got to do with parking lots?"

Carmine bumped Nick's elbow.

"Nick is getting a little bit ahead of himself. The attraction was the scientist's invention, The Black Box, a device to re-energize executives like you all over the world. It only required standing by the box once or twice a day. I think the offering said that the invention had to do with ions. Now, mind you, the scientist, a very honest man, said the device was experimental. He needed money for R&D. You know, research and development. The brokers liked the risk, and they got the most out of it. A few months after the offering was sold, they regrouped. I believe they either paid out or kicked out the scientist and went into the parking lot business. That's how it happened."

Nick smiled. "I'll say. That's a smart way to start a business, wouldn't you say, Mr. Greco?"

Ray turned to Sol. "Mr. Katz, I haven't heard from you. Do you mind reducing this proposal to facts and figures?"

"Sure. The boys need one hundred thousand dollars in venture capital. With that money, their clean record, and some research, my broker and a team of lawyers will underwrite Research Unlimited for at least one point seven million dollars. In return, you'll get your one hundred thousand dollars plus interest and options, netting about three times your initial investment. If you don't want to hold the paper, we'll tell you when to jump ship. . . . Your return is guaranteed."

"All that is well and good. But no one has told me what Research Unlimited does, or what it would do with the one point seven million besides paying me back. Do you have a real business plan?"

"What difference does it make what the company really does at that point? As long as it offers a good risk factor, most investors will buy. At this stage, the more we explain the more we take away from the risk factor. And the boys' plan offers plenty of that."

A quizzical look from Ray was enough to get Nick going again. This time, though, Nick got up and closed the door, walking back slowly. "Mr. Greco, a few months back Carmine and I were playing golf with two guys from South Africa and we got a solid lead on a few possible oil spots. We only need seed money. When the new issue is sold, we'll go down there for a month or two, shoot a couple of probes, and document the operation with photos and reports. If we come out dry, we close shop, come back home, and invest in something that can pay salaries for everybody. That includes you, too, Mr. Greco."

"What about the stockholders?"

"Well, that's the way it goes. Win a few; lose a few. What do you care? By then, you got your money back plus."

With nothing more to learn, Ray rose to his feet, nodded in gratitude, and then pointed them toward the door. "You have an interesting proposition, gentlemen. I'll call Joel in a few days."

Ray never made a business decision on the spot. On this occasion, though, no sooner had Sol shut the door behind him, than he grabbed the telephone.

"Hi Joel, Ray."

"How did it go?"

"Joel, I have never been so tempted to kick someone's ass out of my office. Sol's got those guys so screwed up, it's pitiful.

"From what I learned today, and I'm glad I did, you mean to tell me that as long as the facts are somewhat disclosed in the offering with some half-assed disclaimer, crooks can go public?"

"Uh-huh."

"Well, regardless, I learned enough already."

"I'm sorry, Ray. Sol is a friend of a friend, and I don't think he'll get far with that mind-set. Besides, the bottom just fell out on new issues, too many scams."

Victor called on Ray at half past twelve. "I hope I'm not too early."

Ray shuffled papers in his outgoing box. "Funny you should ask. Traffic must be light. Everybody seems to be running early today."

Victor looked on and smiled. "Let's do lunch."

"Okay, let's grab a sandwich at the Jewish deli around the corner. They got the best cuts money can buy."

From their booth, they watched people rushing by on the crowded sidewalk. Corned beef for Victor and brisket for Ray. Both sandwiches on rye with mustard, French fries, green pickles, and Coke.

"Listen, Ray, true, I spent seven years spinning my wheels on the Coast. You and I go back a long way, and I think we can be frank with each other."

"I don't mean to hold anything back from you, Victor, but you know how it is. When you care for someone, what's in your heart should never reach your lips. And my heart has been heavy since my father was killed."

"I know that, and that's honorable, but there are other things I'd like to know. What's going on with the Class of '56 and Don Saverio?"

Ray looked out the window again. "Do you remember when he warned us about the Mafia meeting in upstate New York?"

"I do."

"Well, he busted that meeting. His people tipped a local cop who got the FBI. That's how far he went to put the old Mafia out of business."

"If you ask me, Ray, he did more than bust those guys. As I recall from all the media accounts, he exposed the old Mafia bosses for what they really were—anything but organized. He sent a strong message to the old boys to quit, and to those who admired the old Mafia to stay away from it."

"And that was the beginning of the end."

"You know, I often wonder why he went through all that. What did he get out of it? It makes no sense."

Ray spread more mustard on his half-opened sandwich. "Victor, Don Saverio in a strange way is the ultimate con man. He got all he wanted and more. While he tempted us with the so-called glamorous lifestyle of Mafia, for when you're young and stupid, that's all you think about in Sicily, he got us in school. He knew that educated people would rarely have anything to do with old Mafia. He is the living proof. It was a brilliant con job: He never asked us to do anything illegal. He not only made it an absolute condition, but he shielded us all from the old Mafia."

"I still don't see what he got out of Mafia reform, Ray."

"My take is: Besides getting himself out of the muscle Mafia, he got a legacy of new Mafia that will live forever in politics and big business. Its doctrine will shape men and women as leaders of substance and honor."

"Ray . . . what's the Class of '56's final objective?"

"First, let me clarify a very important point. The Class of '56 is not a bunch of derelicts on a journey to unattainable goals. Each member is a doer dedicated to a higher cause than himself. That includes you, regardless of how you feel about the California deal. It was beyond your control. You'll do everybody a favor if you stop blaming yourself. You were dealing with a sophisticated con artist who had all the hallmarks of a lawful businessman, that's all.

"Second, those doers and all the others who followed in their footsteps free from political constraints will continue to spread Don Saverio's ideology. It will rise to all levels of leadership, across continents and under the flag of democracy, for that is what captivates the oppressed.

"Democracy will thin out into a chaos of rules and regulations. It will become an ideology without substance that cannot stand alone, no less lead the masses it captivates.

"In the background, only our people will have the substance to guide and get leaders of their choosing elected."

Smiling, Ray tipped the waiter, got up, and led Victor out of the deli. On their way back, there were no talks, only deep thoughts.

Back in the office, Victor sat at one end of the coffee table and Ray at the other trading thoughts. "Ray, what you said about doers at lunch rings true with me. Don Saverio used to tell us how dangerous the non-doer's philosophy was to the doers. In the past, there were geniuses who made life-changing contributions to the human race, and yet most were scorned. We prosecute them, put them in jail, and even lynch them. All because of the non-doer's fear of what these achievers represent.

"No penalty man can muster, including death, will ever erase a doer's deed. His deed will live forever. On the other hand, take away the money from the non-doer and what's left? Nothing. Zero. They leave no imprint whatever."

Ray sensed Victor's passion for the subject.

"Mind you, Victor, some doers come to us as creators and others as leaders. The most effective doer is the one with both qualities. This unique breed I call Professional Dreamers. They are capable of seeing, creating, and taking that vision into reality."

"Ray, I agree. Except that I call your Professional Dreamer, Champion. The creator or the doer is the guy who swims upriver while everyone else swims downriver. The greater the challenge, the harder he swims. He wants no credit, just enough money to keep on going. He wants the world to reap the benefits of his creation.

"The leader, on the other hand, takes a doer's creation and brings it to fruition. The Champion or, better yet, the CEO is the guy who makes things work from start to finish. He envisions, creates, and delivers. And when he has to make things happen, he reaches deep down inside and finds that extra something that others can't."

"Well, Victor, who do you think we're talking about?"

Victor, taken back, said nothing.

"You went to the Coast and got let down, Victor. In those five years, dozens of start-up companies achieved great successes and are still growing thanks to you. They are testimony to your achievements. If that doesn't qualify you as a CEO, I don't know what does."

"Ray, I appreciate your words. But I need more experience than you're giving me credit."

"To some extent, you're right. However, let me give my short version of what makes a CEO. And we're talking about a productive CEO, not like those slick con men I met this morning."

"Who?"

"Some swindlers . . . The only things these people are seeking are extra payment through cockeyed bookkeeping, insider stock deals, and, I'm sure, tax evasion. After they rip off their investors, they don't even show an iota of contrition. Some of them get a weird satisfaction and even brag about it. They're just scum without conscience. They should be thrown in jail for good. But that's their problem . . . getting back to us.

"A productive CEO is a person who works all sorts of hours, sacrifices his family, celebrates no holidays or birthdays, and doesn't take a day off, much less a vacation. He puts work ahead of pleasure. He promises to someday make it all up to his family and to whatever friends he has left. And when he thinks the job is done, he finds another frontier to conquer. A productive CEO is that person who is not afraid to roll up his sleeves and get down to work, a person who thinks he can do better even after the job is done. A productive CEO doesn't accept mediocrity. He has no other rationale. A productive CEO has the guts to learn from his mistakes and try again and again until he breaks through. In answer to your question, Victor, a CEO with those qualities has an innate gift that no hands-on experience can ever deliver. You don't make that kind of CEO. Each is born with the talent and passion to be one. As they say, either you have it or you don't. And in my book, Victor Como has it all."

Victor smiled.

"What do you think is the difference between a productive CEO and a con CEO?"

"We could talk for hours on that subject, Victor, but let me just add this. A con CEO's main objective is to get power through wealth. He can be seen showing off on yachts, at resorts, and in all sorts of extravagant ventures. Some of them are discreet, others not. Like the non-doer, the con CEO feeds on others, always scheming to get more, even if getting more means the destruction of the company he runs. He's always treading on thin ice with his associates and stockholders.

"On the other hand, a productive CEO's life is moderate. His main concern is how to make things better for the enterprise he leads and for those who depend on him. He's the least concerned with personal wealth, as wealth is the by-product of his good efforts. Nor is he concerned about losing his job, for he solidifies his position with every challenge he undertakes."

Victor, like all others who tried to dissuade Ray from the argument and had failed, admiring him, said nothing.

"Now that we agree, Victor, let me tell you what's on my mind. Shortly, I'll have a business plan I want you to look at. It has to do with electronic modules for devices that will facilitate the billing process. They tell me this technology will revolutionize the credit card and computer businesses. If you like it, I want you involved. In the meantime, Pat can use your help. He's reforming Giglio's production team. What do you say?"

"Sure . . . I'd love to."

21

BRENDA POURED HERSELF A SHOT OF WHISKEY and jerked it back. The alcohol stopped her shivering. Not knowing if the General was coming up to spend the night, she got ready anyhow. She unbuttoned her blouse, took off her skirt and bra, and sat at the bar in her panties. She would slide them off before he came through the door. He liked to find her naked and ready. Perhaps the thought of her being naked, alone, and waiting for him was all he needed to get excited.

Their arrangement was simple. He paid for every Wednesday night, and when he brought guests along, he paid double for each guest she entertained as he watched. He usually parked the car by the road and climbed the stairs to her chalet. As long as she got paid, it made no difference whether he showed up alone or with an army: The more the merrier, she always thought.

The General was in his late sixties. He was a handsome, gray-haired man with a craggy face, rigid posture, and a commanding manner. He was used to having his orders obeyed, and, for the money, she was very obedient.

When Sal and two other men came through the side door, she was stunned. She watched as they surveyed the apartment.

Brenda was blonde with blue eyes, fleshy lips, and a capricious face.

146

Her breasts were large and firm and tipped with big rosy nipples. She wore black panties with a red heart embroidered on the front.

Sal tossed his raincoat on the sofa. "What's your name?"

Scared and expecting the worst, she inched toward the window that overlooked Bern. She was hoping to see the General coming up the stairs. There was no General; nor did she answer Sal. The closest chalet was a good mile away and the city fifteen minutes down the road. In the dark of the night, she could barely make out the cathedral's tower.

The elder man looked at Sal. "I don't think she can talk. Maybe I should take her into the bedroom and—"

"Look, guys, don't get any ideas. Do as you're told. Check the rooms and leave the girl alone."

Then he turned to the girl. "I don't care about your name; just get dressed, and if you know how, make some coffee. We'll be here for awhile."

Under the gleaming eyes of the three men, she rushed to put on her bra, blouse, and skirt. Somewhat relaxed now, she turned to Sal. "I'm Brenda; what are you looking for?"

"Nothing."

She sat on the barstool. "Then why are you here?"

Sal sat on the other stool next to her. "We came to surprise the General. We're good buddies. We know all about his tricks. Just relax; everything is going to be okay."

"If you're his buddies, how come your friend wanted to take me to the bedroom? That's not friendly."

"He just couldn't wait. He didn't know the General likes to watch that sort of thing."

Sizing up Sal's friends, she was already spending the extra money she would earn. So, she cheerfully went off to make coffee.

Sal watched Brenda come back smiling with a full pot of coffee and a half-empty bottle of whiskey.

"Brenda, what you don't know is what the General really likes."

"And what's that?"

"A real surprise; it never fails. Every time he gets so excited that he can go with three girls at once for hours, so give us a hand."

"Sure. What do you want me to do?"

"Chain the front door. When he knocks, wait for my cue. Then let him in without saying we're here."

"Shucks, that's easy."

She reached for the bottle.

"Not yet!"

Sal took the bottle away. "Wait until the party starts, all right?"

She chained the door and went back to her stool, crossed her legs, and looked down at her swinging foot quietly. The three men were on their third cup of coffee when a car stopped under the window. The elder man stepped out the side door. A key unlocked the front door. The General rattled the safety chain.

"Brenda, let me in."

Sal waved her to the door.

"Why all dressed up?" complained the General, as they walked into the living room.

"Who the hell are you? . . . This better be a joke." The General's thoughts of taking both men single-handedly quickly faded when he heard the front door slam shut and saw a man with a fake smile standing behind him. The General accepted his invitation to sit down.

Sal poured him a cup of coffee.

"Calm down, Dan, we're friends. Have some coffee, and let's talk things over."

The apartment changed into a courtroom where verdicts are delivered in minutes and sentences are carried out on the spot. Sal and the General sat at the coffee table with the two men, the jury, playing cards at the dinette table behind the sofa. Brenda, the sole spectator, was mystified as she watched the trial from the bar. The General, knowing the predicament he was in, had no choice but to listen. Sal presided over the case.

"Let me ask you, Dan . . . do you know Victor?"

"Oh my God, I can't believe this. I told him . . ." He looked around to anchor himself. He hesitated then smiled. "Tell him I'll take care of it next week when I get back to the States."

Sal rubbed his jaw line. "Dan, I'm afraid we can't do that."

"Why's that? My word is good; ask him."

"It's not a matter of asking. You see, Victor's out. I bought your account, and we're here to collect."

"Okay, okay!" He pulled out a checkbook from his coat pocket. "Sooner or later, let's get it over with." With pen in hand and ignoring the piercing stares from the card players and Brenda's occasional glance, he looked at Sal. "Two hundred and fifty thousand . . . right?"

"Wrong. Two hundred sixty-five, plus thirty-five collection fees makes it an even three hundred."

He handed Sal the check. "Okay. You got what you came for, please leave now."

Sal looked at the check and found a disparity with the bank account number Ray had sent him. "Not yet, Dan. . . . What's the hurry? There's plenty of coffee in the house to last us until the bank opens tomorrow morning. Make yourself comfortable, my friend."

"You mean my word is no good?"

"Your word is as good as this check is, and it better be good. Trust me, Dan. You don't want those two butchers on your back."

The General paused, looking deep into his cup as beads of sweat began rolling down his neck. "What if I get you two hundred fifty thousand dollars cash?"

"Three hundred, now. Three fifty in one hour, and fifty thousand for each additional hour after that."

The General glanced at Brenda who was looking at Sal passionately. "Okay, okay, three hundred it is. I'll be back in an hour."

"You never give up, do you, Dan? They'll go with you."

"Why? . . . Well, okay."

"Don't play stupid; I'll wait one hour."

Sal looked at his friends. "They got orders, Dan."

No sooner had they left than Brenda approached Sal and got down on her knees. Staring at the ceiling, his only excuse was that she was too good. Guilty about cheating on his wife, for the next hour he dismissed the encounter as a job-related hazard. At twelve sharp, exhausted, he pulled out a nylon string from his belt. Kicking Brenda off him, he jerked her head back and wrapped the string around her neck twice like a rodeo cowboy tying the legs of a calf. He pulled hard, until she struggled no more. He never got to know her last name.

The trio got the cash and left Switzerland by train, heading south. The next morning, the FBI issued a report: General Dan Kohaski, unable to cope with a pending investigation, hung himself.

22

IT WAS AFTERNOON, and for Ray this Sunday was almost over. The ride back home, from Manhattan to Scarsdale, was a breeze as it had been in the morning. Thanks to the remote control, even the parking was easy. With the box of souvenirs and the old Olivetti in the trunk and Silvana by his side, Ray thought about starting his novel away from Mafia. Silvana, on the other hand, thought about fulfilling the role of matriarch away from business. Their future seemed bright.

Annoyed by the article, "The Last Gasp?" and happy at Silvana's early return from London, turning his thoughts to the man in the elevator, Ray decided to forgive the kid from Harman Street. After all, he wasn't a kid any more. Ray had given up on that sort of thing.

He unloaded the car and set the box on the floor and the Olivetti next to his computer. Staring at the typewriter and the computer, he thought, *the odd couple*, and smiled. He rolled up the yellowed paper one notch and typed: "Thanks Ma."

The tic-tic-tics drew Silvana's attention. She approached, but could only read the two familiar lines. The third one was illegible. The ribbon had dried out.

A Z C V M M Q

R a y G r e c o.

"_ _ _ _ _ _ _ _."

Ray read them clearly.

Silvana stepped back into the living room and smiled. Going through the souvenirs, Ray's memory ignited. He saw the many events that led to the demise of Don Saverio.

The first memento was a twenty-five-year-old newspaper clipping. It showed a gasoline station with a car at the pump. In the forefront, there was a large sign—Gasoline by Appointment Only. That clipping had marked a turning point for Ray.

In 1973, OPEC hiked oil prices and curtailed production. Giglio's contractors followed suit. Between these two groups, however, there was a distinction. The oil lords strangled a world grown reliant on cheap oil for money. Don Saverio Cremona strangled Giglio not for money, but for his own survival. As Don Saverio's plan to topple Mafia families came toward fruition, so did Ray's plan to topple him. While Don Saverio depended on the moles to come back home, Ray depended on Sal stopping them from ever getting back. Weakened, Don Saverio fell in a power struggle with his daughter and Ray.

Silvana grew to hate her father for what he had done to her family, in particular the slaying of her brother, Stefano. Ray's hatred also continued to grow, not only because of his father's slaying, but also because Don Saverio had impeded his dreams of becoming a novelist. And both hated Don Saverio for what he had in store for their family and Giglio. For Don Saverio, the struggle was for the survival of his cause. To achieve that goal, Don Saverio exerted power on Giglio through its contractors.

In the late spring of '73, Silvana was still angry with her father as she tried to cope with Giglio's problems.

"Whatever it takes, Ray; we must stop him."

"Easier said than done."

"I still can't believe it, my own father?"

"Your father is so wrapped up in traditions that he'll kill his own mother if he had to."

"So, what's next?"

"Nothing, I'm meeting him next week."

The scenic drive from the airport to Alcamo became progressively riskier with each mile. To Ray's regret, the road was as torturous as it had been in 1956. The American highways had spoiled him. To keep the safety factor on his side, he ordered the cabdriver to pull over and get out of the cab.

"Now, listen . . . you! I have a mother to visit, and I intend to get there in one piece. Now, if you know what's good for you, you'll follow my rules."

"What rules? Do you see any white lines or markers on the road? There are no speed limits here."

"I understand. Here's twenty dollars, and here are my rules: Never exceed twenty miles per hour on curves and forty on straight-aways. Never pass horse-and-buggies or any other moving object in a blind spot. Break those rules, and not only will I take the cab and the money back, but I'll also kick your ass all the way home. . . . Is that clear?"

"We'll never get there."

"You let me worry about that. Just follow the rules."

"You're the boss."

The ride took an extra thirty minutes.

The best twenty dollars I've ever spent, Ray thought as he got out.

The cab sped away.

Once a year, Ray would come to visit Don Saverio for the usual one-on-one talks. This one was unusual, as it was the second of the year.

Before going to see Don Saverio and after a pleasant dinner with his mother and Sal, the two men took the customary stroll men take down the *corso*. At the sidewalk café, they ordered two espressos and watched others strolling by.

"What happened to the General?"

"He was an asshole. He hung himself."

Ray stared at Sal and said nothing.

"Look, Ray, if the boys did it, they would have taken the rest of the cash. Read the papers. The hotel room was stashed with cash."

Ray understood.

"What about the girl?"

Sal blushed.

"When the General failed to come back, she had to go."

"I'm meeting Don Saverio in the morning."

"I guessed that much. What's wrong?"

"Nothing's wrong. Just old business, he's suspicious."

Sal pushed the cup to one side and leaned forward.

"Listen, Ray . . . let's get it over with."

"Not yet; maybe by year's end. Right now he has too much of a squeeze on us. Pat and Victor are replacing his contractors as we speak."

"Then we're set. Year's end it'll be."

"Don't pin me down. Before I make a move, I want Silvana firmly on my side."

"Okay, I'll buy that, but what's with these suspicions?"

"Don Saverio thinks I've wised up to him."

"What do you mean?"

"Lately he's acting like a wounded beast."

"Well, let's see. How would you feel if besides losing your sons and more than half of your moles, you had to rely on your son-in-law whose father you killed?"

"I know. But I don't think my father troubles him a bit. To him, the killing was justifiable business, no different from having Stefano killed by Carlo. I bet what's killing him is not being sure about me; otherwise, I wouldn't be here talking. But he has to worry about his daughter and grandchildren."

"What makes you think he's suspicious?"

Regarding the crowd of strutting Don Juans strolling up and down the *corso*, Ray looked at Sal with trust. "When I first left in 1956, Don Saverio and I talked about my father's accident. I don't think he ever bought my story. He gave me a short spiel assuring me it was an accident. Back then, all was well. Carlo was alive, his troops in top shape, and I was going to lead the new enterprises, so he brushed the whole thing off. At least I thought so."

"I guess father and son never took into account the work of fate."

"Without their help, I don't think fate would have worked the way it has so far."

"Does he have any inkling about your plan?"

"Yes and no. He can't prove a thing, since I've been loyal to his plan. When I took over Carlo's job, I followed his plan to the letter. Now with his men fading away, he's getting more suspicious. Soon he might stir up something before I'm ready to act."

Sal enjoyed the last drop of coffee. "I think you're right. You can't afford to wait another ten years. Your grandfather always told me, 'Never take too lightly Mafia's ability to regenerate.' After World War II, Don Saverio built a legacy of *mafiosi* all through Sicily. In Palermo, Castellammare del Golfo, Calatafimi, Camporeale, and Corleone, he was the central figure in the formation of their families. Believe me, Ray; he can rebuild an army quicker than you think."

"Not that easily, or as fast as you think. He has to justify his change of heart about old Mafia and then reposition himself. And the new generation is not apt to follow someone as blindly as their ancestors did."

"You don't think he can regenerate?"

"I didn't say that. If anybody can, Don Saverio definitely can. He has enough money to motivate not just a town but a city. That's not what he wants. Do you remember the kid from Harman Street? You bought him for a dollar more than I did. You can buy services, not loyalty. And don't kid yourself; he knows that too well. Anyhow, Sal, let's call it a night, and I'll see you tomorrow afternoon."

As they walked back home, Ray leaned his arm over Sal's shoulder. "Before I go back to New York, I would like to take some photos of the gravel plant."

The driveway leading to the villa hadn't changed much in the last seventeen years. The trees had grown; two rows of evergreens shaped to waist-high walls had been added to each side of the walkway. They did not hide the old light posts. Older and grayer, Don Saverio stood at the north window as usual, ready for a new day. Two young guards disguised as gardeners were edging the greens.

"Good morning, Mr. Greco."

"Good morning." He walked into the house and thought, *Who the hell are they? I've never seen those two characters before.*

Looking at the marble staircase, Ray sensed loneliness. No one else lived in the house but Don Saverio and his wife. With his right hand on the banister, Ray looked up and smiled at Donna Maria, who had just appeared. He watched her come down the stairs. At the bottom landing, instead of pestering him about Silvana and the children, she held his hands. "Please, be patient with him."

He kissed her forehead and hugged her gently. Then he began to climb what felt like the longest flight of stairs. The door was ajar. Don Saverio, still looking out the window, mumbled, "Women."

"Yes, and only God knows what He had in mind," Ray said, reaching for his chair.

"Good morning, Ray, please sit down."

"Don Saverio, she's a good woman."

"She's my wife . . . "

Ignoring the tradition that women should never interrupt business, Donna Maria brought in a fresh pot of coffee, homemade cookies, and a heart full of pain. But she couldn't speak her mind. She was sorry for the intrusion. Then, like a tornado, she swirled out of the room in her long black dress.

Both sensed her desire to will peace between them. As men of honor, they stared at each other. There wasn't much to say but to accept their positions in a game of fate.

Don Saverio was sixty-seven and Ray thirty-six. Both had aged since their first meeting in that very room. Ray saw lines of frustration on Don Saverio's face and thought, *Perhaps that's what made Donna Maria leery.* They got down to business.

"Don Saverio, lately I have been having problems with six of my contractors. Unless I do something quickly, they'll put Giglio out of business."

"Are you asking me if I'm aware of it?"

Before he could answer, Don Saverio handed him a list. "Let's be sure. Do you mean these guys?"

"Yes, those guys."

"Ray, let's not play games this morning. We both know why you're here, so let me put you at ease. I own a majority of each of those companies."

Ray nodded.

"I'm buying them outright, and there's nothing that you and Silvana can do to change that."

To Ray's surprise, Don Saverio had just set him free from Mafia traditional rules, but he wanted to reinforce that claim. "What about the children?"

Don Saverio smiled. "Who do you think I'm doing this for? I want you and your family back here. Giglio is a drop in a bucket compared to what I have put together for you all. Tell Silvana not to worry. I'll take care of everything."

"I'm glad you told me. I'll tell her. I'm sure she'll appreciate what you're doing for us."

"No, she won't. She's as stubborn as a mule. You are the man of the house. Do what you have to, and for God's sake, put some sense into her. I told you once, don't piss away your future. Your family belongs here now."

Either the man's crazy or he's playing the best con job ever. "What about Giglio?"

"What about Giglio? For all I care, you can shut it down. Without me, it ain't worth a dime." Then he paused to compose himself and half-smiled. "With your know-how, you can fry much larger fish here."

"I see what you mean."

Deaf from the bout, Ray thought, *Father and daughter partners, just the way he envisioned when he first promised to back her up. Get Ray to bring her and the kids back home, get rid of Ray, and groom the kids for the good of the family, even change their last names to Cremona. Why not? Blood is blood.*

Both men reached for some water. Each was in his corner, refreshed, and ready for another bout. Don Saverio was cordial now.

"How're the boys?"

Hoping to get a better read, as he was not too sure of Don Saverio's end game, he followed the course, but was not direct with his answer. "Don Saverio, as you said, we are not going to play games, nor do I want to disrespect you. Allow me to tell you where I think we are and where we are going with the new enterprise. As for the old Mafia, as you well know, we have made serious inroads. In the last five years, we have toppled more than half of the families. John DeMaria thinks that within ten years the job will be done. Anyone left standing would be irrelevant, and greed will take care of that. They'll wipe themselves out sooner than we think."

Don Saverio walked back to the window. "Well, those are our enemies. What about our friends?"

"The Class of '56 is doing well on both fronts: business and politics. Those who followed, I believe a little more than three hundred so far, are working well with the rest of the boys. They are achieving their goals faster than we expected."

"From what I read in the papers, there is no question that most ethnic groups are now coming on board."

"Indeed they are. When you think of what they teach nowadays about political and business leadership, it amounts to nothing more than Mafia; it's a philosophy that will spread into all branches of leadership. In essence, Mafia is an innate trait of those who lead."

"What do you think the future holds?"

"A leader, to spread a message, thanks to television, radio, and print news, won't have to beat his drum at every corner to reach just a few. Using the media, he can move masses in favor or against a person or a principle across continents. It only takes a single message of fear or hope, or convoluted news-spin, if you will. Through the media, leaders can collude with other leaders without incriminating themselves. They can issue talking points without ever meeting with subordinates, staffers, or supporters. Just watch those world leaders, warlords, business tycoons, and every other two-bit thug taking advantage of the system already; not to mention the Vietnam War, the Nuremburg trials, and political campaigns. Through the media, every pundit and reporter will express his opinion, not news. As I said, to advance their agenda, the media will also promote ideological writings that will set off the masses."

Looking out the window, Don Saverio listened to Ray proudly.

"We're approaching unprecedented times. Mafia is finally reaching the hearts and minds of those who want to lead. The kind of Mafia I'm talking about is a global codebook of advanced political and business rules to help balance different democratic views. It is a code of silence

giving leaders that special character needed to make responsible decisions, regardless of personal or political cost, especially when faced
with the extremes of those views. Above all else, this code tells them
how and when to move toward the center."

"If I ever erred, Ray, it was in my weakness for your perceptions. As
you know, I thought of new Mafia back in 1945. Then, in 1956, when
you called it a new enterprise, I went along with it, for the new Mafia
wasn't advanced at all back then."

"How can I forget? I bet you still have that clipping with Stalin,
Churchill, and Roosevelt right there in your drawer."

Don Saverio nodded.

"Although your dream came true, let me tell you where I think
your new Mafia is headed. For starters, we're losing our identity
and influence. Most newcomers don't even know your name. Nor
do they feel obliged to respect those who paved the way and to
make—"

Don Saverio's stare cut Ray off. "That's exactly what I want. All
within the rule of law, no strings attached to old Mafia. As you know,
back in the fifties I started an educational program. I instigated a ma-
nia for emigration here that's still going. The goal was to spread a new
Mafia, while shaking off the old Mafia stigma for Sicilians. To that
end, I didn't care who spread our ideology, as long as it took hold. We
started in the United States because with the separation of church and
state there, people can be persuaded more easily than in any other na-
tion. But remember, only through honorable men of substance can the
masses truly benefit from our ideology."

As he spoke, Don Saverio's stern look sent chills down Ray's spine.
For a moment, he wished he could embrace and trust him again, but,
focusing on his own agenda, he thought, *No wonder he didn't care whether his men ever came home. In fact, he might be very much relieved at not
having to explain his true position to anybody.*

"Ray, what do you think happened to Joey and those other guys
who signed up with the FBI?"

"The only thing I can assume is that . . . is that freedom and
education are a volatile combination. Once you set a man free, he
seldom comes back. In a way, it's not much different from you leav-

ing the muscle Mafia for the pencil Mafia. Until we learn who we are and what we truly want, we are prisoners of circumstances and fate."

The grandfather clock was about to strike noon. For the first time, Ray was the one to end the meeting. "I think we can make things work. In fact, I'm meeting with my plant manager in less than one hour. I'm flying back home this afternoon. If we put our heads together, we can supply every cubic yard of ready-mixed concrete for every highway built from here to Rome and beyond. By the way, we just put a new mobile gravel plant on line. Next time up, I want you to see it in operation and give me your input."

On his way to meet Sal, Ray recalled a point of wisdom his father had taught him, "To catch a pair of tuna, you must land the female first, for the male will stick around fighting for her until death." Don Saverio wanted to catch Silvana back home.

It was well past two, the start of the traditional two-hour lunch. Accustomed to Sal's tardiness when occupied with mechanical challenges, Francesca asked her son to call for him; lunch was on the table. Ray drove the short distance to the gravel pit. When he pulled into the parking lot, he stirred up a white ball of dust that engulfed the car and all else around it. When the dust settled, Ray could see Sal on the crusher a little way up the hill behind a sign that read GRECO ROAD MATERIALS AND CONTRACTING. He was working on the latching system for the deck railing.

"Sal, let's go; lunch is getting cold!"

Sal rushed down the small winding road. "Oh my God, what time is it?"

Ray patted Sal on the back. "What's the difference? Let's go. We're late."

"I tell you, I have done this too many times. One of these days, she's going to kick my ass out. I tell you, I'll deserve it."

"I didn't mean to rush you, but I'm taking off in a couple of hours. We're having a special meeting tomorrow afternoon; things are getting hectic back home."

"How did you do?"

"The man is so entrenched in his plan that he's ready to squash anybody in his way."

"What's with all that stuff we talked about?"

"We were dead wrong. The only thing I can guess is the man doesn't give a hoot about anybody, least of all the moles. You have to understand that when his father died, he was forced to quit college. He never accepted it, since he was on his way out of Mafia. And although he ran a tight ship, with the streak of vengeance of a traditional Mafia boss, he was always looking for ways out. Obsessed with the idea, he spent most of his life reforming Mafia. Now, much like his daughter, he's completing his dream. Both father and daughter are trapped in a senseless feud, and neither one is much satisfied with the likely end game."

"What about your end game, Ray?"

Ray patted Sal's back once more. "I guess I'll have to come back sooner than I thought."

23

IN THE WEE HOURS OF THE MORNING, a limousine pulled up on the tarmac of Westchester County Airport. It was winter, and it was cold. As promised, Ray had called Silvana one hour before he landed. Picking each other up at the airport had become a symbol of their devotion.

All bundled up, she looked at the tower for the double flash. The air traffic controller conspired in their love affair with telephone calls and flashing lights, signaling the plane was on final approach.

Rolling down the runway, the jet swallowed the cold air. With engines hissing now, Ray felt each bump along the way. The sight of taxiway lights slipping under the wing relaxed him. The fear of flying had never left him, especially during landings.

What troubled Ray tonight, though, was his meeting with Don Saverio. He was wondering about how he had misread him all along. But what bothered him most was how much he agreed with him and how committed he was to his philosophy.

Nevertheless, the more he tried to shut off the bad thoughts about the meeting, the more he heard Don Saverio saying, "I'm buying them outright, and there's nothing you and Silvana can do. . . . I want you and your family back here. . . . She won't understand. . . . Put some sense into her. . . . Don't piss away your future. . . . Get rid of Giglio."

Although troubled, Ray was certain that once on solid ground, with Silvana and the children by his side, he wouldn't need to make any new commitments, just fulfill the one at hand.

Ray exited the jet briskly as Silvana ran toward him. They met on the apron and hugged as if they had been parted for thirty years rather than three days.

The driver packed the luggage into the limousine and started the fifteen-minute ride home. Silvana cuddled up closer to Ray.

"Ray, I think I know . . . he wants to take over Giglio."

Ray shook his head slightly. "You are as wrong as I was about his muscle power. He wants you back home."

"You must be joking?"

"No. I am not."

"When hell freezes over. I'm not starting that again. I tell you, Ray, I've had it. We have to break away for good. This is it. The man will not listen to reason."

"There's no need to get all uptight. Silvana, that's his problem. We'll do what we have to do."

The turn into the driveway calmed them both.

"We're home; we'll talk over breakfast."

Fed, composed, and ready to go to school, the kids lined up in the vestibule waiting solemnly. Aunt Laura was outside warming up the station wagon. When Rex barked, the orderly trio broke up and ran after their father. They all screamed and barked at once.

"Mommy, Mommy. Daddy!"

"Woof, woof!"

"Mommy!"

"Woo-oooof."

"Mommy! Daddy, Daddy!"

Teary-eyed, they told their awful tales of troubles in school. Comforted by hugs, kisses, and presents, they smiled at Aunt Laura who was waiting patiently. Then, with a stern but warm look, she called them into the wagon. Little Francesca waved with a mitten dangling off her wrist and a smile as they drove away.

"Ray, are you ready for breakfast?"

"Not really. I traveled all night. We have a two o'clock meeting downtown; I'll put it off to four. I want to spend some time with the kids when they come back. What do you say?"

"I'm sure they'll love it."

"Okay then. I'll take a nap, and we'll have brunch instead."

By the time Ray came down the stairs, brunch was ready.

He poured coffee. "Looking at those kids today, I can't imagine them growing up anywhere else."

"I told you already. I'm not going, nor is the rest of this family. Let's forget the whole thing and do what you have to, quickly."

"There's nothing to do but to stay put until Giglio frees itself from those bastards. Victor and Pat have worked on this plan for quite some time now. I think we can switch before Easter."

"Did you make up your mind on how to do it?"

"Somewhat. We'll talk at the meeting."

"Okay, we switch . . . then what?"

"Then I'll deliver the news to your father myself."

"What kind of news?"

"I'm not going to shoot him. I'm going to have one more man-to-man talk. That's all."

Silvana looked the other way.

"By the way, I think you are terrified at the idea of going back."

"Don't be silly, Ray. I can live in Alcamo or any other place I want. But I won't raise my children where their future is slated. No. I won't do it."

"Neither would I. But for now, let's keep it to ourselves. I need some time to get ready for the meeting before the kids get back."

Trusting in his judgment, she cleared the table as he withdrew to his study. For reasons Ray never understood, Rex was very quiet when the kids were not around.

They crossed the Triborough Bridge.

"Ray, if you were wrong about the muscle power and I was wrong about him taking over Giglio, what's his game?"

"Your father controls those contractors. The way he sees it, to get us back to Sicily, he has to put Giglio out of business."

"That's terrible! How can he do that knowing how I feel about my career?"

"Not according to him. In fact, he wants to do more for you."

"I guess, without Carlo, our kids are the only blood left for him to mold, huh!"

"As I said, he wants Giglio shut down and me talking you into going back. For that, he'll give you all he owns, which according to him, makes Giglio a drop in the bucket."

"What did you say?"

"I told him it was a good idea and that I'd talk you into it."

"Yeah, right!"

The limo turned southbound on East River Drive.

He's my father, after all, the man who understands me. I did say someday I'd pay a price for it, didn't I? A barge coming up the river blasted its horn twice and broke her thoughts.

"Well, Ray, you talked to me already and you know how I feel. But I haven't heard a word about you, Mr. Greco."

"Well, that's another matter. I'm sure your father has something good in mind for me, too, wouldn't you say?"

Wisely, she said nothing. She knew this was a time to support her man. Ray was her only hero now.

At twenty minutes to four, the limousine pulled up in front of the office building. He instructed the driver to come back at six. Gabriella smiled, as if she was on her first hour of work and not her ninth and counting. "Welcome back."

"Thank you, Gabriella. Is everybody here?"

"Everybody but Sergio; he'll be here shortly."

At a glance, Ray could tell they had been working hard to solve problems. The octagonal table, although polished, showed overuse. There were pads of paper spread about and binders out of place. Giglio was behind in its delivery schedules. Despite repeated follow-up calls to the contractors, it was losing ground. There were not enough goods being shipped. The situation demoralized the team, the staff, and merchants alike. Ray saw the table as a battlefield where his dreams were dying.

When Sergio came into the room, Ray called the meeting to order. Except for some remarks taken on the fly, Ray had reached the decision alone, in the privacy of his mind. No one, not even Silvana, was privy to it. He shot friendly glances at his team. "The time has come to kick those bastards out. We'll do much better without them. I'll tell you how."

Pat, Sergio, and Victor were thrilled. They had worked for some time getting things ready for this day. Silvana, who had been consumed by the thought of going back to Sicily, suddenly felt like a death-row prisoner set free. She wasn't the only one. Gabriella, eavesdropping from her office next door, applauded the news. Unbeknownst to them, Ray was also relieved. With his team, he found the courage to decide. Don Saverio's threat no longer loomed over them.

The team took a five-minute break while Gabriella, who thought she was jobless a minute earlier, reorganized the table neatly and brought out new refreshments. She thought it would give a fresh start to the team.

Back at the table, Ray looked at Victor, Pat, and Sergio. "I know I shouldn't say this, but it's too critical to our survival. Therefore, I must insist that whatever we discuss here remains here. Any leak could easily send the whole deal tumbling down like a house of cards."

Understanding his concern, they nodded.

"To outsiders, we'll tell things that only benefit us. Please, trust nobody. Above all, don't fall for hearsay stories or trade reports. Our success depends on the secrecy of the plan. Giglio has no money problems. As a company, it enjoys an excellent credit rating, and it has ample cash reserves. Giglio's problem is production. As anticipated, our new marketing plan sparked more sales, outgrowing production tenfold. To make things worse, our friends have not only curtailed supply but also refused to tool up for the increased demand. Don't ask me why. Those are the facts. I believe they have an agenda of their own. Therefore, the first thing we'll do is sign up the replacement contractors."

He turned to Victor, "Did you check them out?"

"They're all clear. . . . But as Pat suggested, we should create some kind of partnership with these fellows. Little more than a cold-cut relationship would do. These are good people ready to work hard at a moment's notice. Contrary to our friends, they are seeking steady orders and willing to chip in for advertising costs."

"That's refreshing, Victor. You're right, but maybe down the road a bit. We need time before we venture into that kind of partnership. I'm aware that no relationship can last long unless the deal is good for all parties. To that end, our basic deal is good. For now, we have to approach the switch orderly. Provided they sign an agreement promising to keep their mouths shut, we sign them up for next season. Then we'll tell the old boys we are going out of business. We promise that if they keep their mouths shut, they'll be well paid, because we are working on a bankruptcy scam."

"Why should they care whether we go out of business?"

"Sergio, Pat, Victor . . . please listen. I don't know why. The plain truth is they want us out of business. For now, they got us in a squeeze, and if we don't give in, they'll squeeze even more. So, I tell you what we'll do. To buy time, we'll tell them we're going out of business, and because Giglio cannot afford any bad publicity or a total production shutdown, it behooves us to keep our mouths shut, too."

Sergio looked at Ray. "I didn't mean to question you, but it's just unfair."

Silvana cut in. "Sergio, Pat, listen. Victor and I were born in Sicily and understand Ray's thinking better. I guess if he was at liberty to do so and if it helped the company, he would lay it all out. I trust him. I hope you do, too."

"Do you really think that those bastards, on a promise alone, will up production?"

"I know so, Pat."

"When do we start?"

"Now. Sergio."

A week after the meeting, Pat and Ray were having lunch at the Jewish deli.

Pat smiled. "Production is up."

"What did I tell you?"

24

RAY ARRIVED IN ALCAMO the day before the festival. With time to spare, he drove to Torre Saracena atop Monte Bonifato. With a bird's eye view of the city, he studied the scene, recalling the history of his native land. As a teenager, he came up here often to think. Never before did he face so few choices. Facing north, Ray could see the thousand-year-old Alcamo on a plateau some two thousand feet below.

Alcamo, once the ancient Arab city of Alqamah, is nestled in the slopes of Monte Bonifato. The topography of the land encloses and secures the city, as there is no natural access to the mountain from the south. The east and west ends of town are protected by two artificial gateways: Porta Palermo and Porta Trapani, interconnected by the mile-long Corso 6 Aprile, Alcamo's main street.

From Porta Trapani, the *corso* forks into two roads: the Lower Road and the Upper Road. They rejoin some fifteen miles out of town. The Lower Road leads to Alcamo Marina, the new train station, and Calatafimi. The Upper Road leads to the Carrubbazzi, the old train station, and Calatafimi as well. Porta Palermo, built a few hundred feet above the eastern landscape, is the gateway to Palermo.

Ray felt Don Saverio's attraction to the city when he looked out of his window. Don Saverio often lost himself in the historic myths and truths of the land and its people. It shaped his character. The seemingly liberal Don Saverio was a man of deep-rooted conservative convictions. As Ray found out, he would go to any extreme to preserve that philosophy.

Once a year, Alcamo holds a festival for its patron, the Madonna dei Miracoli. The three-day festival takes place in June. For the event, booths that sell cotton candy, straw hats, toys, and more, pop up all over the crowded main street. Sideshows offer games of darts, loops, and cards. In short, it is a carnival that excites even the city's most conservative hearts in a spirit of celebration of miracles yet to come when they lift the Madonna through the streets.

For the afternoon, the *corso* becomes a mile-long racetrack. They spread sand and stretch ropes through waist-high posts on both sides of the street. At race time, people line up against these ropes like reeds on riverbanks, several layers thick. Those residing on Corso 6 Aprile watch from second- and third-floor balconies.

At the blast of a shotgun, the horses dash out from Porta Palermo and under steady whipping, race to the finish line at Porta Trapani, where the horses must be stopped in the shortest possible space—another race in itself.

The strong spectators, foolishly, get to show off by grabbing and dragging themselves on the horses' necks. Even though year after year many of them get hurt, some badly, every race has new takers for this lunacy. The viewers from the balconies, besides watching the men being dragged like punching bags, enjoy the mile-long body wave caused by the spectators below.

At the sound of the shotgun, they lean forward and then quickly back again as the pack of horses race by, only to lean forward again for a glance at the horses' tails as they speed toward the finish line. This wave effect mesmerizes those viewers above more than the race itself. As the people below disperse and mill about the sideshows, the people above stay put on their balconies waiting for the next race to start.

After dining with his mother and Sal on Thursday, the last day of the festival, Ray waited in front of the church for the procession to start. It was a crowded scene with people full of hopes. He had promised Silvana he would march alone and barefoot, something most believers do at least once in their lifetime. This was Ray's time.

When in need of help, most natives of Alcamo, other than Don Saverio, pray to the Madonna of Miracles. They can do this anytime and from anywhere in the world, for she is their hope and conciliation. To entice her to answer their prayers, believers promise the Madonna a penance, money, or some other offering.

For the good of his soul and a hope to restore his life on track, Ray promised the Madonna the penance of marching alone and barefoot. Dressed up casually with a hooded windbreaker, he joined in the cheers and bowed as the Madonna came into view. She had an aura of bright lights and a myriad of colorful rays radiating from behind her into the sky. The sight brought believers and nonbelievers to their knees. Her calm and reassuring expression was framed by a blue mantle trimmed in gold amidst hundreds of flickering candles. The apparel made her look more like a live being than a statue on a throne.

Twelve faithful carried the throne complete with flowers and two large pinup boards for money offered. The leader carried a bell with a wooden handle that signaled each stop and go. One ring for stop, two for go. To make it easy on donors, the procession stopped often along the way. The throne slowly headed east on the *corso*, preceded by the city band and followed by the mayor, the bishop, the chief of the municipal guards, other dignitaries, and thousands of followers.

The procession filed out under the weeping eyes of what seemed to Ray like millions of people. They used the same ropes that had fenced the racetrack earlier, only this time they went the other way toward Porta Palermo. On the second stop, they came up to the city's intellectual nerve center, the Cultural Club, Alcamo's most menacing place for the illiterate. The club hosted several jobless professionals. These folks philosophized about life all day long, sometimes for years, waiting for the right job, rather than trying life by taking any job. Although most members were top scholars and active thinkers, they too were philosophers and as such had no interest in the hard facts of life, making money. Ray felt as indifferent as Don Saverio did about this place.

One stop ahead, they reached Cinema Esperia. Ray recalled memorable scenes shown here featuring Bogart, Sinatra, Elvis, Sophia, and other greats. These scenes showed other worlds and lifestyles, shaping the minds of the young and enriching the gossip of the old. Such was the case with the showing of the permissive film, *La Dolce Vita*. For years to come, the young copied the hero, played by Marcello Mastroianni. There was also a rumor that Don Saverio had gone north once to spend a weekend of lovemaking with the voluptuous Anita Ekberg. Ray believed Don Saverio whenever he said it wasn't true. Then again, Don Saverio was smiling every time he said it, and Ray didn't mind his secrecy on that subject.

The bell rang twice, and the procession moved forward. For fear of being seen by a suspicious face he had spotted earlier, Ray pulled up his hood. By now, the band had played enough uplifting tunes that people had stopped weeping. At the Church of San Tommaso, Ray's fear abated when he sighted Sal and his mother.

San Tommaso, the smallest church in Alcamo, was closed for services due to its old age. Completed in the fifteenth century, it was uncertain whether its foundations were first laid in the fourth or fifth centuries. Its main entrance draped with acute arches engraved with rich stone embroidery revealed the artistic styles of the times, inspiring artists like Silvana. The architecture, the sculptures, and the frescoes of these churches—and there were a dozen in all in Alcamo—were the envy of most neighboring towns. Don Saverio often bragged about it at the Class of '56's meetings.

Ray never walked more than a quarter of a mile a week. With shoes on, he walked from the house to the car, to the office and back. Barefoot, he stumbled from the bed to the bathroom, and sometimes to the refrigerator. Well beyond their limits, Ray's walking muscles were aching. His bare feet were blistering. But a promise is a promise, and in spite of the pain, he marched on. When they reached Porta Palermo and turned right, there was Ray's middle school. Here, Ray had discovered girls.

Long gone memories were brought back in a sweet thought of a girl named Assunta. He had been passionately in love with her, although she hadn't noticed. Then there was Silvana. In that school, there were no mixed classes. Boys and girls could not mix or talk, especially in the streets, without a chaperon.

Advancing uphill, the procession didn't stop until well after it reached the level road to the right. Here, the bearers and the band, especially the trombone and the drummers, took a rest. Ray's feet were bleeding now and his heart pounding fast. The more he thought about his heart, the faster and louder it pounded. The fear of having a heart attack numbed his feet and deafened him. He could no longer hear the band, only his heart beating. Ray thought the torture had to be part of the forgiveness without recourse, or a first timer would quit at the first feeling of pain. They traveled west, and as he had hoped, the sidelines thinned out some, but not enough to let the breeze in to cool his feet.

The view of the old *torre* signaled the next stop. Like the churches, the castle had been built in the fourteenth century. It followed the various stages of Alcamo and world history. With its circular, square, and rectangular towers, the architectural structure showed it to have been a fortress, a dwelling, and a prison all at the same time. Its true name was Castello dei Conti di Modica, at one time owned by powerful barons. Over the centuries, the castle had housed kings as well as passersby. It also housed Don Saverio's ancestors, who had shaped political ideas that were still the cornerstone of politics and big business. Perhaps this was the birthplace of Don Saverio's philosophy, thought Ray.

To display the absolute power of feudalism over men and things, the castle was isolated and south of the "farm." With the end of feudalism in 1812, the castle fell into the hands of the community, which, not knowing what to do, used it as a prison as late as 1965, causing it to decay. Today, the restored castle could reclaim its status as a symbol of economic growth in a city famous for its rich artistic heritage; its tourist attractions of the mountain and the sea; and its renowned white wine.

In that moment, Ray was proud of Don Saverio's accomplishments here and abroad. A visionary genius without boundaries, Ray thought, a true champion, willing to go to any extremes to force his will on others in order to protect the continuity of his tradition.

Stepping on a bunch of sharp pebbles, he cracked more blisters open. He limped to the next stop with nothing to hold him up but a cane-like stick handed to him by a sympathizer.

Reaching the mouth of a descending road, Via Giuseppe Mazzini, Ray could see the café down below and to the right, where a few years back Benito Campo had gunned down Carlo Cremona, his two protégés, and then himself. The thought of that tragedy made the noble thoughts Ray had for Don Saverio seem repugnant and more so when he thought about his own father's tragedy.

When they reached the famous café, Don Saverio wasn't there, nor was there the usual empty table reserved for him. The carnival people were busy planning their next stop on what used to be Don Saverio's table, something that neither Carlo nor any of Don Saverio's men would have allowed.

As a true believer in the Madonna, Ray went on in spite of the agonizing pains and cramping muscles. A short left and a quick right took them across the *corso*. From here, they aimed for Via Roma, which, after another left, took them to the west end of town. Two more lefts got them back down the main street again, just about where they had started.

When they first crossed the *corso*, Ray felt sand under his feet. This was the sand used to aid the horses on the track earlier in the day. Hoping to stop the bleeding for a while, he scuffed sand with his toes to fill the cracks. But the sand didn't help much, since the half dozen bleeding cracks were too wide to fix.

Amazingly, walking Via Roma was a breeze. Ray's heart returned to a regular beat, at least until they hit the *corso* homebound. To Ray's astonishment, there was Grandpa, staring at him sternly from the crowd. Wrapped in a black cape, he wore a large hat with a single feather to one side. His mustache was gray and awesome. Grandpa reminded him of the promise he had made on his father's grave. Taken by surprise, he looked down only to hear himself saying, "I'll get them; I promise I will." When he looked up, Grandpa had vanished—he had died five years earlier. Ray couldn't recall what happened from the moment Grandpa vanished to the moment the Madonna of Miracles was safe at home.

His feet were no longer bleeding or cracked. They were smooth and tender. In fact, they were in the best shape ever, and so was his soul. He was at peace.

On Saturday morning, Ray found Don Saverio by the window. The city had quieted down as things got back to normal. It was a beautiful sunny day, June 23, 1973.

"Good morning, Ray. How was the procession?"

"A breeze."

Ray poured himself a cup of coffee. Don Saverio looked out the window then at Ray. "How is she?"

"I think she welcomed the switch."

Don Saverio approached the desk. "What switch are you talking about?"

"The older the kids get, the greater Silvana's passion for motherhood is. Her career comes second now."

"That's an inborn reaction for mothers. What I mean is how did she take the closing down of Giglio?"

Ray, as if resigned to fate, took a deep breath. "As you know, there is so much one can take and then there is the future of the kids to worry about. Silvana has had enough, especially since we decided to file for bankruptcy. Silvana and Aunt Laura are excited about wrapping things up for their trip back home."

"I'm glad she realizes where home really is. Everything will be fine, Ray."

Ray nodded.

"What's the schedule?"

"September, before school starts."

"Real good, Ray. Real good!"

"In the meantime, as I said last time, I want you to look at my gravel operation and tell me what you think of it."

"You're really set on this deal, aren't you?"

"That's the only way I'll move back here. I have to be my own man, you know that."

"I can't fault you for that; it's what honorable men do. Okay. I'll tell you what we'll do. We'll go to the Carrubbazzi first to see your operation; from there, we'll take a quick ride to Calatafimi. I haven't seen

Don Nardo in a long time. I have a hunch; I would like to see him one last time. I was told he's sick!"

The mention of Don Nardo and Calatafimi brought Santo to mind, but Ray knew that with Silvana and the kids on the other side of the ocean, he wouldn't dare make a move.

"Sure, that's good. I'd like to visit Don Nardo, too. It's only a twenty-minute ride down the road, if that."

Don Saverio was in deep thought.

The noise level at the gravel pit was louder than the horn in Ray's car. The gravel pit was in full operation. Half a dozen dump trucks were lined up for loading. Two front loaders were dumping large stones into the chute. Three sets of conveyors were carrying crushed stones into their respective gravel pits. It was an organized chaos of men and machines. Already an hour after lunch, the morning quota was yet to be reached, and the workers were getting frantic.

Kneeling and testing the safety rail that protected the crusher's mouth, Sal was watching the machine devour the large stones. Failing to attract Sal's attention, Ray and Don Saverio, with the help of his cane, found their way between the fast-moving equipment and up the slope to where Sal stood.

When Ray and Don Saverio got onto the deck, the noise level was so high that gestures replaced talking. Don Saverio leaned on the railing to watch the attraction. The operator, who could see the safety latch open, screamed at the top of his lungs:

"Get back . . . get back!"

Sal and Ray jumped off the deck. The rail gave way. Don Saverio dived feet first, letting out a roar that quieted the site into a deafening silence. The operator stopped the spindle and held Don Saverio snug with the upper jaws of the crusher.

Except for Don Saverio, everyone could see the bloodstained gravel flowing toward the pits with shreds of cloth and flesh. The snugness of the hydraulic jaws below his waist kept him alive, holding the blood from rushing out. Sal, who had replaced the distraught operator, kept them still.

In shock and feeling no pain, Don Saverio looked up at Ray. "You got me!"

"It's business." Ray knelt within reach.

"You got Santo . . . too?"

"Uh-huh."

"But . . . why?"

Ray shrugged.

"In case you haven't noticed, my bottom half is gone. As soon as Sal lets go, I'm gone. How about playing it straight?"

"I met Santo a few years back." Ray glanced at Sal, noting his hands on the control panel.

"I always liked your style. You cover your tracks. Never admit a thing. You are not closing your business, are you?"

"No."

"I bet Silvana and the kids are staying in America . . . right?"

"Right." Ray glared at Don Saverio. "You don't get it, do you? My kids—like my father and grandfather—are Grecos . . . not Cremonas . . . can you accept that?

"You not only had my father killed over a stupid road diversion, but you planned to kill me, too, just to get my kids."

"Listen . . . " Don Saverio gripped Ray's hand, his face grimacing in pain. "You have a great imagination. I adopted you as my sole heir long before I killed my two sons. Fate made me kill your father, and I have no other account except that, as much as you resisted Mafia, you were slated to carry out its cause."

Ray flinched.

"Very few men understand Mafia. As to women, the closest they get is to understand the men in it."

Ray realized why he admired Don Saverio. Through him, he understood that Mafia is a gift of life and fate for those who live by it.

"By the way, Ray . . . under the flag of justice, leaders kill. That is the way man protects men from men. Some kill in wars, others on street corners. And so they kill. . . . They always do."

"But why, even your own?"

"It's heredit . . . ar . . . y . . ."

His head slumped back.

Ray pulled his hand away.

With a promise kept, Ray left Sicily. At home with his family and the Olivetti by his side and reams of paper to be filled, Ray began fulfilling his lifelong dream, at last.